Candy Cane Caper

by

Kathi Daley

With Bonus Novella

I want to thank the very talented Jessica Fischer for the cover art.

I so appreciate Bruce Curran, who is always ready and willing to answer my cyber questions and Peggy Hyndman for helping sleuth out those pesky typos.

And, of course, thanks to the readers and bloggers in my life, who make doing what I do possible.

Thank you to Randy Ladenheim-Gil for the editing.

Special thanks to Jeanie Daniel, Pam Curran, Taryn Lee, and Sharon Guagliardo for submitting recipes.

And finally I want to thank my sister Christy for always lending an ear and my husband Ken for allowing me time to write by taking care of everything else.

Books by Kathi Daley

Come for the murder, stay for the romance.

Zoe Donovan Cozy Mystery:
Halloween Hijinks
The Trouble With Turkeys
Christmas Crazy
Cupid's Curse
Big Bunny Bump-off
Beach Blanket Barbie
Maui Madness
Derby Divas
Haunted Hamlet
Turkeys, Tuxes, and Tabbies
Christmas Cozy
Alaskan Alliance
Matrimony Meltdown
Soul Surrender
Heavenly Honeymoon
Hopscotch Homicide
Ghostly Graveyard
Santa Sleuth
Shamrock Shenanigans
Kitten Kaboodle
Costume Catastrophe
Candy Cane Caper

Zimmerman Academy The New Normal

Tj Jensen Paradise Lake Mysteries by Henery Press

Pumpkins in Paradise
Snowmen in Paradise
Bikinis in Paradise
Christmas in Paradise
Puppies in Paradise
Halloween in Paradise
Treasure in Paradise – *April 2017*

Whales and Tails Cozy Mystery:

Romeow and Juliet
The Mad Catter
Grimm's Furry Tail
Much Ado About Felines
Legend of Tabby Hollow
Cat of Christmas Past
A Tale of Two Tabbies
The Great Catsby
Count Catula
Cat of Christmas Present – *November 2016*

Seacliff High Mystery:

The Secret
The Curse
The Relic
The Conspiracy
The Grudge

Sand and Sea Hawaiian Mystery:

Murder at Dolphin Bay
Murder at Sunrise Beach
Murder at the Witching Hour

Road to Christmas Romance:

Road to Christmas Past

Special Note:

This book has two parts. Part one is a NEW Christmas novel entitled *Candy Cane Caper*. This is the twenty-second installment of the Zoe Donovan series.

Part two is a free bonus novella that was originally published with the title *Zimmerman Academy New Beginnings*. I am sharing it with you again so that those of you who have not had the opportunity to do so can read it if you wish. I never plot ahead, but my instinct tells me things may become complicated between Phyllis, Will, and Ethan in the future, and these short stories set up the conflict.

Candy Cane Caper

Chapter 1

Thursday December 15

"So what do you think?" Levi Denton, one of my two best friends, grinned as he held up a black jeweler's box with a diamond ring nestled inside. I'd run into him while out doing some last-minute errands in preparation for the end-of-term Christmas party my husband, Zak Zimmerman, and I were throwing for the students of Zimmerman Academy before they all headed home for their month-long break.

"You bought Ellie an engagement ring?" I asked. "Rudolph the Red-Nosed Reindeer" blared in the background of the crowded department store as holiday shoppers pushed and shoved their way down the crowded aisles packed with merchandise specifically displayed to attract them.

"I wanted to get her something special for Christmas."

"Yeah, but an engagement ring?"

Levi's smile slipped just a bit. "You don't think she'll like it?"

"It's beautiful, but…" I looked around at the throng of shoppers rushing about in the overcrowded store. The environment was anything but the sort in which one would want to have a serious discussion that involved engagement rings. "How about we take a break from shopping and grab a beer?"

Levi's smile faded altogether. "You don't like the ring."

"I do." I grabbed Levi's arm and started toward the front of the store. "It's just that we both know things are a bit more complicated than simply finding the perfect ring."

For those of you who haven't been around as of late, let me catch you up. My two best friends, Levi Denton and Ellie Davis, have known each other since kindergarten. Levi, Ellie, and I have been part of a best-friend triad for almost twenty-five years. Three years ago Ellie realized her feelings for Levi had grown beyond the parameters of that best-friend paradigm, and a year after that my two best friends officially became a couple. A year ago they realized that there were problems in their relationship that didn't seem to have an easy solution, so they decided to go back to being just friends and split up.

The breakup was hard on both of them. Despite the fact that they truly loved each other and always would, some relationships, it would seem, just aren't meant to go the distance. It took a while, but they both seemed to have moved on, and then five months ago, in a moment of weakness, Levi and Ellie found themselves in an encounter of the romantic kind. Ellie soon realized she was pregnant and two months ago she finally told Levi the secret she was terrified would destroy their relationship forever.

You see, the "big" issue that had split Levi and Ellie in the first place was that she wanted children very much and he was quite clear that he didn't want children—*ever*. When Ellie found out she was pregnant with Levi's baby we both feared he'd totally freak out, but the truth of the matter was, once he got used to the idea, he not only was okay with it but it seemed he was actually excited about the baby's arrival.

"I know things are complicated, but Ellie is going to have a baby. My baby. I want my son to be born into an intact family, with both a mother and a father."

"Your baby will have both a mother and a father even if they don't live together," I pointed out.

"It's not the same. A boy needs his father."

"How do you know you're having a son?" The last time I'd spoken to Ellie she hadn't had the test.

"We had a doctor's appointment this morning. The doctor said we're definitely having a boy. My boy. Ellie and I should be married."

I paused and hugged Levi. "Congratulations. I hadn't heard you'd found out the sex of your baby. I'm really happy for you both."

Levi's grin began to return.

"Now about that beer…" I grabbed his arm again and continued down the crowded aisle.

Once Levi and I had exited the department store I turned to the left and headed toward the local pub. I just hoped it wouldn't be too crowded and Levi and I could find a quiet booth where we could really talk. I knew Ellie was relieved that Levi had not only not been mad about the baby but wanted to be an active part of his child's life. Of course she'd also made it perfectly clear they weren't going to be a couple again just because they happened to be having a baby together.

"I know what you're going to say," Levi began as we walked down the snow-covered sidewalk. As they did every year, the merchants in Ashton Falls had gone all out with white twinkle lights and fully decorated windows depicting various Christmas scenes. "You're going to say Ellie has made it perfectly clear she doesn't want us to be a couple again just because of the baby."

"You're right. That is what I was going to say." I flattened my back against the wall of the building we were passing as a group of boys came barreling down the sidewalk. "Ellie loves you. She always has and I'm sure always will. It hurt her very deeply when the two of you broke up. I know she doesn't feel up to putting her heart at risk again."

I opened the door to the pub. Luckily, there was a small booth in the back that was unoccupied. I took Levi's hand and headed in that direction.

"I'm not going to hurt Ellie again. I didn't mean to hurt her in the first place. I didn't know what I wanted a year ago, but I do now. I want Ellie and me and Peyton Manning Denton to be a family."

"Peyton Manning?"

"I'm just trying out names."

Levi was a high school football coach, so I guess the name choice made sense.

I held up my arm so the bartender would know to bring Levi and me our regular order of beer. It wasn't that we went out drinking a lot, but when we did, we always went to the same place, so the staff knew us and our preferences.

I took a deep breath before I continued. It did occur to me that perhaps I should just stay out of the whole thing and let Levi and Ellie work out their lives between the two of them, but if there was one thing Zoe Donovan Zimmerman was not, it was a bystander in the game of life.

"I know you're excited about the baby. I can see it clear as day. But you have to understand that until a couple of months ago you adamantly insisted you didn't at any time want to be burdened by a child. It would make sense for Ellie to think the commitment you feel toward her and the baby will fade once the reality of dirty diapers, sleepless nights, and puke-stained shirts sinks in."

"I would never bail on Ellie and baby Eli."

"Eli is too close to Ellie," I mused. "It would be confusing. How about Tom Brady Denton?"

Levi made a face that clearly communicated his lack of enthusiasm for the name. Brady was the name of the man Ellie had sort of been seeing when the pregnancy occurred.

I placed my hand over Levi's. "I hope you know how happy I am that you're excited about the baby. I know your acceptance of the situation has put Ellie's mind at ease as well. But I really think you might want to let her set the pace on your status as a couple. I really do love the ring you picked out, but it seems to me Ellie is still trying to get used to the idea of being a mother when she never thought she could be. I'm not sure she's ready to deal with the idea of being a wife as well."

Our conversation paused as the waitress brought our beer.

"So you think I should wait?"

"I really do. Let her see that your commitment is real and you won't bail when the going gets tough. Be there for her now and eventually she'll begin to trust that you'll be there for her always."

Levi let out a long breath. "Okay. I know Ellie talks to you a lot more than she talks to me, and I know you want us to work it out as much as I do, so I'll take your advice for now." Levi touched the jacket pocket where he'd stashed the ring. "Of course now I need a Christmas gift that says something more than *let's be pals* but less than *will you marry me*."

"Jewelry is good, but not a ring. Maybe a necklace or a bracelet."

Levi didn't look convinced.

I looked at my watch. "I need to run over to that new bakery down the street to pick up the cupcakes for tomorrow's party. If you want to come with me and help me stash them in the backseat of my car, I'll brave the department store again and help point out some things that I think Ellie might like."

Levi smiled a sort of half smile that both conveyed his disappointment with and acceptance of the situation. "Okay. That sounds like a deal. And maybe you can help me pick out something for Jerry Rice while we're there."

"Jerry Rice?"

"Wide receiver for the 49ers."

"I know who he is." I took a sip of my beer. "If you really want a football name how about Brett Favre?"

"Ellie already vetoed it, along with Joe Montana, Tony Romo, and Odell Beckham."

Levi and I continued to discuss various football-related names while we finished our beers. When we were done Levi paid the check and we headed down the street to the bakery, Candy Kane's Bakeshop.

"It looks dark."

I frowned at Levi. "I spoke to Candy this morning and she said she'd be here until eight. It's only seven-fifteen." I cupped my hands around my eyes and looked in the window. The seating area and bakery counter were deserted and the lights at the front of the shop were dark. "It looks like there might be a light on in the kitchen," I informed him. "Let's go around to the alley to see if the back door is open."

It was a good thing Levi and I both had snow boots on because the path leading from the front of the shop back to the alley hadn't been shoveled after last night's storm. The town had recently been by to plow the alley, however, so once we left the walkway at the back of the property the roadway was clear. We walked down the alley to the back door and knocked. When there was no answer I tried the knob. It turned. I slowly opened the door and stepped inside the warm interior of the building.

"Candy? It's Zoe Donovan. You told me to stop by any time before eight to pick up the cupcakes."

"It looks like the place is deserted." Levi observed.

We looked around the kitchen and then went through the double doors to the front of the store, which was still dark.

"That's odd. Why would she leave the back door unlocked if she had to leave?"

"Maybe she just forgot to lock it," Levi suggested.

All the lights in the kitchen area were on and a quick check of the industrial-sized oven verified it was also on. There were cookies and cakes cooling in the racks and a bowl of cookie dough had been left out on the counter.

"Maybe she just had to run out to her car or next door or something quick," I suggested.

Levi pushed open the door to the walk-in pantry. "I don't think so. It looks like you'd better call Salinger."

While I was waiting for Sheriff Salinger to arrive I made my way to the front of the shop to see if the cash register had been tampered with. The obvious motive for murder in this case seemed to me to be a robbery gone bad. The cash drawer was closed, but when I hit the Enter key to open the register I found it empty of cash. It was possible Candy had already cleared the money from the register for the day, but if she hadn't, it looked like a robbery was most likely the motive for murder. It made sense to me that someone had entered through the back as we had, thinking the shop was deserted and the door had been left open by accident. When the thieves had entered the kitchen they'd heard Candy in the pantry and hit her with a rolling pin, which, based on the fact that there were sugar cookies on the cooling racks, would most likely have been sitting on the counter. Of course there wasn't a rolling pin in sight now, so at this point that was just a theory.

I opened the drawer beneath the cash register and found a little notebook, along with a stack of handwritten receipts and order forms. Realizing that knowing who had been in the bakery prior to Candy's death could provide an important lead, I grabbed both the notebook and the receipts and headed back toward the kitchen just as Salinger was coming in the back door.

"It looks like someone hit her over the head with a rolling pin, a bat, or some similar-shaped object,"

Salinger informed us as he knelt next to Candy Kane's body and examined the evidence before him.

"That's exactly what Levi and I decided. Given the fact that the pantry looks to be undisturbed except for the presence of the body and the puddle of blood on the floor, it doesn't appear there was a struggle. Someone must have come up behind her and hit her before she even knew she had company."

"I think you're probably correct. The crime scene guys are on the way, but with the snow and traffic it could be a while," Salinger informed us. "If you want to answer a few questions for me, I'll let you go on your way."

"How long has she been dead?" I asked.

"Hard to say until the medical examiner gets here, but I'd say Ms. Kane has been dead for less than an hour. Why is it the two of you happened to be here when the store was clearly closed for business?"

"I was supposed to pick up cupcakes," I explained. "Candy told me she'd be here until eight, so when we arrived and saw the store was dark I looked in the window. When I saw the light was on in the kitchen we came around to the back. The door was unlocked and the lights and oven were on."

"Whoever did this must have accessed the shop through the alley," Salinger stated. "Did you notice anyone there when you arrived?"

Levi and I both answered that we hadn't.

"It looks to me like Candy was the victim of a robbery gone bad," I stated. "The cash drawer is empty. I checked while we were waiting for you. I suppose it's possible she'd already emptied the cash drawer, but I don't see a deposit bag. She could have taken it to the night drop at the bank."

"I can check with the bank. When did you last speak to Ms. Kane?"

"This morning. On the phone."

"And how did she seem?"

"Happy. Almost chipper. I think in spite of everything that has been going on with the bakery down the street, business has been good."

"The bakery down the street?"

"Candy just opened this shop a few months ago. I guess that put a kink in the business that bakeshop had previously enjoyed. I don't claim to have all the details, but I've heard from some of the folks in town that Veronica of Veronica's Bakery convinced some of her more loyal customers to boycott this place, even though Candy was offering better prices. There was quite a bit of mudslinging between the two. I'm not sure if they ever worked it out, but Candy seemed to be busy, so I'm guessing there were enough folks who wanted to take advantage of Candy's prices to keep her going."

"Do you think Veronica would have killed Candy over their rivalry?"

I frowned. "I hope not. I don't know Veronica all that well, but she doesn't seem the sort to kill someone for encroaching on her business. You might want to talk to Gilda over at Bears and Beavers. She's friends with Veronica. I suppose she might have more insight into what Veronica is or isn't capable of."

Salinger jotted down a few notes. "Anything else?"

"I found this." I held up the notebook I'd found while we were waiting for Salinger to arrive. "It looks like it's a list of all Candy's customers. There are names and phone numbers, as well as notes on everyone's favorite pastry. I also noticed Candy seemed to have assigned everyone a customer number. I thought I'd look through to see if I can figure out who might have been here just prior to the time Candy was murdered."

"I'll take those." Salinger held out his hand.

I shrugged. "Suit yourself."

Salinger asked a few more questions and then told Levi and me that we could go. He promised to call me the following day to fill me in on the status of the case. The last thing I wanted was to be involved in a murder case just ten days before Christmas, but Candy Kane had been a nice woman and I wanted to see her killer found.

Levi and I held hands as we walked back to the car. We'd both been shaken by what we'd seen, but it seemed as if Salinger had things well under control.

"So what are you going to do about the cupcakes?" Levi asked.

"I guess I'll stop at the store and get some mix. They won't be quite as good as cupcakes bought from Candy Kane's bakery, but at this point beggars can't be choosers."

"How many do you need?"

"Ten dozen."

"Wow. Ten dozen? That's a lot. I can come over to help if you want. I'm sure Ellie will be happy to help out too."

The reason I'd ordered the cupcakes from the bakery rather than asking Ellie to make them was because I didn't want to tire her out, but with Zak and me and Levi helping, I was certain we could get the cupcakes whipped up in no time.

"Thanks. I'm going to take you up on that." I glanced toward the department store. "About a gift for Ellie…"

"I'll look for something over the weekend. I have to say, finding a woman dead in her pantry has put a damper on my Christmas spirit."

Based on the number of cupcakes we needed, we decided to use the kitchen at Zimmerman Academy because it had an industrial-sized oven. I went to the store for supplies while Levi went to pick up Ellie. Then I headed back to my house and got Zak and the four of us met at the recently opened school.

Zimmerman Academy had been built as a private school for intellectually advanced students. Due to the short building season in snowy Ashton Falls, we were rolling out the campus in stages. Last year we'd rented a building in town and offered classes for half a day. This year we were open full-time following the first phase of development, which had included classrooms as well as a temporary kitchen and library, which had opened in September. Dorms and a larger cafeteria and library were part of the plan for the next phase of the Academy, due to open next fall.

Still, even the temporary kitchen had appliance capacity and counter space by far surpassing a regular kitchen's.

"You should have just let me do these in the first place," Ellie commented as she mixed up the batter she insisted she had to make from scratch in spite of the fact that I'd bought five boxes of mix.

"You were already making cookies and I didn't want to tire you out," I explained.

"I've been feeling better lately. The morning sickness is completely gone and I have a lot more energy than I did during my first trimester. Levi, be sure to whip the frosting until it peaks. We want it to be nice and fluffy."

Levi saluted her in military fashion.

"By the way, congratulations on having a boy." I stopped what I was doing and hugged Ellie, which caused the mixer to raise slightly, sending cake batter all over the kitchen.

Ellie laughed as she turned it off, then turned and hugged me back. "I'm sorry I didn't tell you sooner. We just found out this morning and I was swamped today, getting the kitchen ready to be closed for a month. I was going to call you this evening, but I guess Levi let the cat out of the bag before I had a chance."

"I understand. It seems like we've all been so busy lately. It's kind of nice having the four of us cooking together, even if the reason isn't so nice."

"Do you want white frosting for all the cupcakes?" Zak asked Ellie.

"I'm going to dye half red and half green. You can start on that if you want. There's food dye in that brown bag on the counter, as well as sprinkles to decorate the tops of the cupcakes after they're frosted."

"These really are going to look nice," I commented.

"If I had more time I'd experiment with fillings, but this will have to do."

"Well, thanks again. Next year I'll just ask you to do the cupcakes in the first place."

"You'd better. In fact, next year I'll have my new kitchen and can just do them at home."

Zak and I were remodeling the boathouse so there would be more room for Ellie and the baby. Part of the remodel was a whole new kitchen.

"Speaking of the remodel," Zak said as he mixed the food color into the white frosting, "I spoke to the contractor today. He said we'll need to finalize all the materials in the next week or two if we want him to start working as soon as the snow melts."

"Materials?" Ellie asked.

"Types of flooring, cabinets, appliances. That sort of thing. I have a bunch of different books for you to look through."

"It's still your boathouse," Ellie reminded him. "Shouldn't you and Zoe pick out the materials for the flooring and cabinets?"

"We're expanding for you and the baby. We want you to feel right at home. The choice should be yours," I insisted.

A single tear slid down Ellie's cheek that she quickly wiped away with the back of her hand. She might be feeling better, but she was as emotional as ever. "You guys are so great. I don't know what to say."

"Say you'll come by to look at the books," Zak answered.

"Okay. I will tomorrow. But I want to pick something we all like, so let's all look at the books together."

"Scooter's dad is coming by in the morning and we have the party tomorrow afternoon, so why don't you and Levi come for dinner and we'll pick out everything then," I suggested.

"Scooter's dad is in town?" Levi asked. "Hasn't it been about two years since he last visited?"

"More than two years," I said. "He's shown absolutely no interest in his son for years and now all of a sudden he decided he wants to be a daddy."

"He's only here for a visit, though?" Ellie asked. "He's not planning on taking him?"

Now I was the one with the tears on my cheeks. "We aren't sure. Scooter's dad has a new girlfriend. He told Zak he was ready to settle down and be a family with his son." Scooter had been an everyday part of Zak and my life for the past two years. I wasn't sure what I was going to do if his dad did want to take him away.

"I guess that's a good thing," Levi said. "The man *is* Scooter's father. A boy needs his dad."

"How does Scooter feel about it?" Ellie asked.

"He's dead set against it. The last time he saw his dad he was a drunk who happily let Zak take over as his temporary guardian. But now? I'm not sure. I guess we'll have to wait to see what happens."

I tried to put on a brave front, but I was really dying inside. Scooter wasn't ours by blood, but in every other way he felt like our son. Still, Levi did have a point. Scooter did deserve to have a relationship with his dad, and if things worked out between them, Zak and I had already decided we weren't going to do anything to stand in his way.

Chapter 2

Friday, December 16

When Scooter's dad arrived the next morning with his girlfriend—who, as it turned out, was actually his fiancée—I wanted to cry. Scooter looked both fascinated and horrified when the buxom brunette wrapped him in a bear hug that put his face against her cleavage.

"It's nice to meet you." I stuck out my hand in an effort to interrupt the embrace.

"You too," the woman, who had been introduced as Brandy, answered. She leaned forward and gave me a quick kiss on the cheek. "What a cute home you have."

"Thank you. This is my husband, Zak."

"Happy to meet you."

I wanted to hate the woman, but she seemed really nice. Nicer, in fact, than Scooter's dad, who had yet to greet anyone, including Scooter. Scooter looked at him with distrust on his face when the man simply looked at him and said, "Son."

Scooter turned to Zak. His expression seemed to be begging him to intervene so he didn't have to go with his dad.

"What are your plans for the day?" Zak asked.

"We're going to the street fair," Brandy provided.

By *street fair* I assumed she meant the Hometown Christmas celebration, which kicked off that day and ran through the weekend. I was sure Scooter would have a good time, and his father's arrival had allowed him to skip the last day of school before the break, so maybe it wouldn't be so bad.

"Am I coming back here tonight?" Scooter asked.

"We'll see," his dad answered.

Scooter looked at me, but all I could do was offer a smile of encouragement. The man taking him away was his dad, who had every right to take him for as long as he saw fit.

"I'll be anxious to hear all about it when you get back." I hugged Scooter as tight as I could and he hugged me back just as tight.

"You'll take care of Digger?" Scooter asked about his dog.

"Absolutely," I answered.

"And you'll tell Alex to stay out of my room?"

"I'm sure she will."

Alex was the twelve-year-old girl who had been in our lives almost as long as Scooter. She was at school this morning and so was missing the painful good-byes.

After Scooter left Zak wrapped me in his arms while I shed a few tears. I wanted Scooter to be happy and I really hoped his dad and Brandy could do that, but somehow I didn't see it happening in the long run.

"It'll be okay," Zak consoled me.

"I know. I'm sure Scooter's dad will do what's best for him." Even as I said the words I doubted it completely.

"We should get loaded up and head to the Academy. The party starts at noon and we still need to set up."

"Okay. Let me just wash my face."

I went upstairs on that pretext, but what I actually did was call Salinger. I'd been anxious to hear from him, and once the party started we wouldn't have much of a chance to chat. Besides, I needed something to distract me from the gaping hole in my heart that seemed to grow exponentially every time I thought of Scooter leaving us for good.

"Donovan," Salinger said after the first ring.

"Salinger."

"Are you alone?"

"I am. Do you have news?"

"I do."

I'm not sure how the predictable banter that began every phone conversation between the two of us had started, but it was a routine we'd grown comfortable with, and to tell you the truth, if Salinger responded in any other way I'd suspect there was an imposter on the other end of the line.

"I'm listening."

"The medical examiner confirmed that Ms. Kane died as a result of blunt force trauma to the head. We didn't find the murder weapon, but as we suspected, it appears to have been a rolling pin or some other similarly shaped item."

"How long had she been dead?"

"Between fifteen and thirty minutes prior to your arrival."

Fifteen minutes. The killer could very well have still been nearby when we got there.

"Any suspects?" I asked.

"A few. I spoke to Veronica from Veronica's Bakery. She admitted Ms. Kane had been a thorn in her side since she arrived in town and that they had engaged in several altercations, a few of which had ended in physical violence, but she claims she didn't kill her."

"Physical violence?"

"She said an argument they'd had a few days ago in front of Candy Kane's Bakeshop resulted in hair pulling and slapping. Nothing more."

Geez. Hair pulling?

"Do we believe her?" I wondered.

"For now, but she's still on my list."

I glanced out the window. It was starting to snow. Again. The giant flakes looked pretty as they landed on the colorful lights Zak had strung everywhere.

"Anyone else?" I asked.

"Veronica told me that Ms. Kane was involved in a dispute with her neighbor. It seems the neighbor has a yappy dog, and Ms. Kane threatened to call animal control if she didn't deal with the dog's barking. Ms. Kane had filed previous complaints and the dog owner was already on her last chance: One more complaint and the dog will be picked up and taken to the county facility. I'm not sure if that will pan out, but I'm looking into it. I really haven't had time to do much follow-up. I'll talk to you again this evening. I assume you planned to snoop around. We can compare notes."

Did I? I wasn't sure. I had a lot on my plate already with the holiday coming up, combined with everything else that was going on. I informed Salinger that I wasn't sure I'd be able to help out with this one but that I'd keep my ears open and let him know if I heard anything I thought might be relevant. I could tell he was disappointed that I was less than enthused about helping him, but he was the sheriff and I was just the sidekick. A very busy sidekick at that.

"This is really nice," Zimmerman Academy's principal, Phyllis King, said to me later that afternoon as the students pigged out on junk food and hung out for one last time before break.

"Are the girls going home for the holiday?" I asked, referring to the three girls who lived with her.

"No, they're all staying in town. We're planning a big Christmas Eve dinner with the four of us, Ethan, Will, and the girls' current boyfriends. I invited Brady and his children as well as Jeremy and his family. It will be potluck if you want to stop by."

"Thanks, but I think we're going to my parents'. How are Will and Brady getting along now that Will has settled in?"

Will Danner was the first math teacher for Zimmerman Academy, until he'd quit the previous January to move closer to his elderly father. Brady Matthews and his three children had then moved to Ashton Falls so he could take Will's place. Will's dad had died during the summer, and Will had called Zak, asking if there were any openings at the school. Brady had been doing a fantastic job and we didn't want to upset that in the least, but Zak felt the Academy could support two math teachers, so he'd brought Will back too.

"They're getting along just fine," Phyllis said. "There was a bit of awkwardness at first, but they have clearly defined roles that ensure they won't be stepping on each other's toes. Once Brady realized his job really was safe he began to relax. It's Will and

Ethan who seem to be knocking heads since Will has been back."

"Will and Ethan? Why?"

"I really don't know. It's the strangest thing. They got along fine when Will worked here before."

I looked around the room for Will, who was chatting with Hazel Hampton. Hazel was both the town and Academy librarian, as well as my grandpa's girlfriend. I noticed that although Will was chatting with Hazel, he was looking at Phyllis. Will was younger than Phyllis, and at the time of his previous employment he'd only recently been widowed, but I knew they had gone out a few times, and I also knew Phyllis had been quite taken with him. I supposed it made sense that Will could still be interested in Phyllis, but I didn't see why that should cause tension with Ethan, who had been good friends with her for years. Unless…I scanned the room to find Ethan, who was chatting with Zak but staring directly at Phyllis. Could we have a love triangle in the making?

"Did Alex mention she needs to be at the community center by nine o'clock tomorrow morning?" Phyllis asked.

"I think she said something to Zak about it." Alex was working on a toy drive for the less fortunate in our community along with Phyllis, Ethan, and a couple of the other Zimmerman Academy kids who weren't going home for the holiday.

"I'd be happy to swing by to pick her up if that would help. I know you have your hands full this year with Hometown Christmas."

"I'm not the chairperson this year, so it isn't as bad as it's been other years, but I do seem to have been volunteered for a lot of different projects. I'll check with Zak and let you know, but I might just take you up on your offer."

"It's not a problem at all. You always seem to be juggling so many different things during the holidays even when you aren't sleuthing."

"I guess you heard about the woman who owned the new bakery?"

"I did. What a terrible shame."

"Did you know her?" I asked.

"No. In fact, I'm not one to indulge in sweets much, so I'd never even met her. I have, however, heard quite a bit about her from a couple of the people who I spend time with at the senior center."

"Really. Like what?"

"I'm sure you remember that before Candy Kane opened her sweet shop there was a quilting store in that location."

"Yeah, I remember: Granny's Quilts."

"It seems, based on what I've heard, that the store owner, a woman named Clarissa Vanderbilt, was forced to close down her shop after losing her lease. Apparently, Candy had offered the landlord a higher rent than Clarissa was paying, which resulted in Clarissa being served with a lease termination letter. Poor Clarissa was only given thirty days' notice and was unable to find another storefront she could afford, so she had no choice but to close down her business."

"How could the landlord kick her out if she had a lease?"

"It started off as a five-year lease, but once that was up it went to month-to-month."

I wasn't one to sew anything, ever, so I hadn't been a patron of Granny's Quilts, but I did know a bit about Clarissa Vanderbilt. She'd first opened her shop seven or eight years ago after inheriting a bunch of quilts from her grandmother. The revenue from the sale of the quilts had allowed her to buy an initial inventory of material and other quilting supplies, and I knew several of the women who attended my book club spent quite a bit of time hanging out at her store, where the local quilters liked to gather and socialize. I had, of course, noticed that Granny's Quilts had gone out of business, but I guess I'd never stopped to wonder why.

"Do you think Clarissa would kill Candy over something like that?" I asked Phyllis.

"No, I don't think so. I don't really know Clarissa all that well, but she seems like a lovely young woman. Based on what I do know about her, I really can't imagine her hurting a fly. Still, when she lost her business there were a lot of women in the community who lost their place to hang out. I'm not accusing anyone of anything, but I feel I would be remiss if I didn't mention it."

"Thanks. I appreciate the information. I suppose it wouldn't hurt to have a chat with Clarissa."

"As long as you're chatting with people who held a grudge against Candy Kane, you might want to stop by to speak to Nick."

"Nick Benson?" Nick was a retired doctor who belonged to the same book club Phyllis and I did.

Phyllis nodded.

"Why would Nick want to hurt Candy?"

"I'm not saying he would. Nick is a good man who spent a lifetime saving lives, so I really can't see him taking one. But Nick did have a quarrel with Candy. It seems he parked in one of the spaces reserved for Candy Kane's Bakeshop when he was dining in town. Candy knew he hadn't bought anything from her, so she had his car towed. It cost him over four hundred dollars to get it out of impound. Nick was steaming mad. Candy pointed out that the space was clearly marked as being for customers of Candy Kane's Bakeshop and that if he wasn't a customer he should have parked elsewhere, while Nick argued that there wasn't any other parking near the restaurant where he was meeting a friend and several of her spaces were unoccupied."

Nick was a great guy, but he was the sort to sometimes feel entitled.

"I have to agree that I don't see Nick killing a woman over four hundred dollars and a minor inconvenience, but I'll have a chat with him anyway. He knows a ton of people in town and if I know him, he probably made sure everyone he spoke to knew what had happened to him. If anyone else had a problem with Candy chances are they shared it with him, and he'd lend a sympathetic ear. I really didn't know Candy other than to order some cupcakes, but it seems she made a number of enemies during her short time in town."

"Yes. I'm afraid she did."

Zak and I had brought different cars to the Academy because we'd had so much stuff to transfer from the house to the party, so I decided to stop by to chat with Nick on my way home. I'd called ahead and asked him if he had a few minutes to talk and he'd said he'd be delighted to see me. I'd asked Zak if he wanted to come along; Nick usually had home-brewed beer to offer, but he wanted to go ahead to start dinner so it would be ready when Ellie and Levi arrived.

"So, what brings you to my neck of the woods today?" Nick asked as he showed me into his home.

"I wanted to chat with you about Candy Kane. I imagine you've heard she was murdered."

A look of genuine sadness came over Nick's face. "Yes, I heard. She was a thorn in my side, but I never want to hear of anyone meeting their maker in the way she did." Nick shook his head, as if to shake loose a thought. "Please come in. Have a seat. I don't know a lot about her, but I'm happy to share what I do know."

"Phyllis filled me in on the towing fiasco. I understand you've been quite vocal about your anger with the way she handled things."

"You don't think I killed her?" Nick had a shocked look on his face.

"No, of course not. I just know that oftentimes if one complains about someone to a friend or acquaintance, if that person also has a beef with the subject of the complaint, they'll voice their own discontent."

"Is that a fancy way of saying folks are likely to join the bitch bandwagon if given an opening?"

"Exactly."

"I suppose I have heard some complaints about the new bakeshop owner. I can't think of a single person who would actually kill her, but there are those who were upset with the way she steamrolled through her life. I'm sure you heard she had Granny's Quilts evicted."

"I heard. I guess a lot of the women who hung out there were pretty mad."

"Mad is putting it mildly. There's a group from the senior center who were actively campaigning to have Candy Kane's Bakeshop shut down. Still, I seriously doubt any of the seniors involved would commit murder. Have you considered that maybe Ms. Kane died as a result of a robbery?"

"I have considered that. Salinger is following up on that angle. I haven't spoken to him since early this morning, so I'm going to assume he knows by now whether robbery was the motive. I guess I should call him to check in before I waste my time doing too much sleuthing."

Nick smiled. "Well, I'm happy for the company. Would you like to taste a new brew I developed? We can chat while you sip."

"I would, but just a small one. I've had your homemade brew and it can be lethal."

The small glass of ale Nick brought me was actually very good and not at all heavy, as some of his earlier brews had been.

"So, other than the quilting circle women, can you think of anyone else who had a real beef with Candy?" I asked.

Nick didn't answer right away. It appeared he was considering my question carefully. "I guess you've already assumed Veronica from Veronica's Bakery isn't thrilled to have a competitor right down the street. Not that I think she would kill the woman over a little competition. Still, I suppose her partner might have a mind to take things to a physical level if pushed hard enough."

"Her partner?" I'd never heard Veronica had one.

"Most folks don't know this, but Veronica's cousin, Kevin Martucci, actually put up the money to open the bakery. She runs the place and is the face of Veronica's Bakery, but Kevin has a financial, and from what I understand, a controlling interest in the enterprise."

I knew Veronica's cousin. He seemed to be exactly the sort to kill a person over a business venture. It's hard to say exactly what it is about Kevin that gave me the creeps. Maybe it was his calculating nature, combined with his icy-cold stare. Kevin owned and operated a retail outlet in Bryton Lake rather than tiny Ashton Falls, and I knew he'd done quite well for himself after he decided to franchise it. I didn't have any proof that he operated illegally, but there were rumors that corners had been cut and under-the-table deals made in the course of building the empire he now owned.

"Kevin does seem like the kind of man who'd kill someone over a few bucks, but the guy is loaded. Why would he care about a rival cutting into the profit margin of a tiny bakery he owns with his cousin?"

"I'm not saying he would. I just thought I'd mention the connection to the bakery."

I thought some more about Kevin and his icy stare. "I suppose I can have Salinger check to see if he was in Ashton Falls at the time of the murder."

"Might be a good idea."

"Thanks, Nick. And thanks for the beer. It was your best brew yet."

"Tell that husband of yours I have a pint with his name on it if he wants to stop by."

"I will." I stood up to leave. "Thanks again for everything."

I called Salinger as soon as I returned to my car. I filled him in on the link between a man who was known for possible shady business dealings and Veronica's Bakery, and he told me Candy hadn't deposited her earnings on the day she died, so a robbery was still very much a possibility. I brought up my discussion with Phyllis and he shared a disturbing piece of news that left me reeling.

Chapter 3

According to Salinger, Willa Walton, a county employee and head of the Ashton Falls Events Committee, had been seen leaving Candy Kane's Bakeshop through the back door just minutes before Levi and I had arrived. Salinger had spoken to Willa, who claimed she'd gone to the bakery to speak to Candy about her business license, which she'd neither applied nor paid for. She'd entered through the back door, which was unlocked, just as we found it, called out for Candy, who hadn't answered, and then left with the intention of following up with her another time. She swore she had no idea Candy was dead in the pantry.

On one hand I really couldn't see Willa killing anyone. Sure, she could be a bit anal at times, with a rigid adherence to rules and protocol that bordered on the ridiculous. And yes, I could see her getting into an altercation of the verbal sort with Candy if she refused to jump through all the hoops required to obtain a business license. But hitting a woman over the head with a rolling pin? That didn't seem like Willa at all.

Salinger agreed with me, but he did point out that leaving a shop unlocked when it was obviously not occupied wasn't a Willa thing to do either. His theory was that she'd found Candy dead, panicked, and taken off rather than calling either him or 911. I wasn't sure how I felt about that. It was true that in normal circumstances if Willa found the shop both wide open and unoccupied, she would have either waited for Candy to return or locked the door behind her. For her to just leave everything as she'd found it was a very atypical thing to do.

The first thing I noticed when I got home and walked through the door was the wonderful smell coming from the kitchen. I really lucked out in the husband department. Not only was Zak the kindest and most loving person on the planet but he's a hell of a cook as well. Which is a good thing because I can barely boil water.

"What smells so wonderful?" I asked Zak after kissing him in greeting.

"Lasagna."

"Scooter's favorite. Is he back?"

Zak paused.

"He's not back?"

"His father wants him to stay with him for several days at least."

I paled. "At least?"

"He mentioned the next few days as sort of a trial for a more permanent arrangement."

I sat down on one of the kitchen chairs and willed myself not to cry. Intellectually, I understand Scooter wasn't our child and we'd only been filling in while his father got his life together, but emotionally, I considered him to be as much my child as any Zak and I were likely to give birth to, and the thought of him being removed from my life left me feeling broken and battered.

I wiped away a single tear and tried for a smile. "I guess that leaves more for Alex, who loves your lasagna almost as much as Scooter."

Zak sat down at the table next to me and put his arm around me. "Alex is spending the night with

Phyllis. They're going to work on that children's book Alex has been writing. I didn't think you'd mind, especially because Levi and Ellie are coming over."

"I don't mind," I said, even though I was feeling fragile. I was proud of the book Alex had written about my dog Charlie and the adventure he took to the North Pole on the Candy Cane Express at Christmastime. Phyllis, who was a retired English professor before she took on the job of principal at Zimmerman Academy, was going to help her find someone to publish it.

Zak pulled me into his arms and kissed my neck. "On a positive note, once Levi and Ellie leave we'll have the house all to ourselves."

I started to cry.

"I'm sorry, Zoe. I know you're worried about Scooter. I shouldn't have tried to make light of it."

"It's okay," I sobbed. "I don't even know why I'm crying." I looked around the empty room. "Where's Charlie?"

"Your parents stopped by. They were taking their dogs to the dog park and took our three with them."

I started to cry again.

"I can go get them if you want."

I shook my head. "No. It's almost dark. I'm sure they'll be back any minute. I'm going to go upstairs and wash up."

I grabbed a handful of Kleenex and headed up the stairs. Geez. Did I ever need to get a grip! I took a deep breath and willed my emotions into check. Levi and Ellie were on their way over. They were going to wonder what had happened to the Zoe they knew and loved if I went down to dinner all weepy. Yes, I was worried about how things with Scooter might work out, but crying over what might happen wasn't going to change anything.

I decided to take a hot shower and change into my sweats. Levi and Ellie weren't going to care if casual Zoe showed up for dinner, and given everything that had happened I felt the need for my comfy clothes. I didn't want to fuss with my thick, curly hair, so I braided it down my back, took one last breath of resolve, and headed down to dinner.

When I arrived in the kitchen Zak, Levi, Ellie, and all three dogs were hanging out waiting for me. Charlie ran over to greet me and I scooped him up for a big hug.

"How's my boy?"

Charlie licked my face in reply.

Of course Bella and Digger didn't want to be left out when they realized I was giving out kisses, so I knelt down on the floor and greeted the larger dogs as well.

"They sure are happy to see you." Ellie laughed.

"Always. You should have brought Shep with you."

Shep was Ellie's German shepherd.

"Levi brought Karloff over, so we decided to leave both dogs at the boathouse. We figured we wouldn't be too late."

"Dinner's ready," Zak announced as he slid a tray with garlic bread out of the oven. "Let's eat before it gets cold. We can look at the sample books afterward."

Dinner was delicious, and having my two best friends in the house seemed to chase away the gloomy mood I had found myself wrapped up in earlier. We actually had a really good time picking out wood for the cabinets and floor and tile for the kitchen and bathroom counters. Levi joined right in as if he planned to be living in the boathouse along with Ellie and the baby, which I guess he did plan to do, even if Ellie didn't know it yet.

Maybe I'd made a mistake telling Levi to wait to propose to Ellie. They both seemed happy and they certainly were getting along. When Levi offered his opinion about the color of the carpet Ellie didn't make a comment about him not living there. Of course choosing a carpet together and entering into a lifelong commitment weren't the same thing, although if you really thought about it, having a baby together was about as big a commitment as they came.

Once all the decisions regarding the remodel were made our conversation naturally segued to the murder investigation I still wasn't certain I wanted to be a part of.

"Wow, that is strange," Ellie responded when I shared with the others what Salinger had told me about Willa. "I really can't see her leaving an unlocked door unattended. Did Salinger tell you what she said about it?"

"She just said she figured if Candy had left the door open in the first place she must have expected to be back in a very short time."

"If that's true why didn't she wait?" Levi asked.

"It does seem like she would have." I nodded. "Willa is like a dog with a bone once she discovers someone is operating outside the system. She'll hound you until she sets things right. I was a few weeks late with my own business license fee one year and she acted like I'd committed a capital crime."

"Her story isn't quite lining up," Zak agreed. "Still, Willa? I don't see her as being the murder-and-run sort. If—and this is a very big if—something did happen between Willa and Candy that resulted in Candy's death, I see Willa calling it in herself."

"Yeah." I shook my head. "The whole thing is strange, but Willa would never kill someone and then run away."

"So if we're all in agreement that Willa isn't a real suspect, what else did you learn?" Levi asked.

I spent the next thirty minutes getting everyone caught up to speed. Considering the fact that I still hadn't committed to investigating this case, I'd learned quite a bit in just one day.

"It seems as if this woman rubbed a lot of people the wrong way," Levi said. "It might be hard to figure out who among the many was rubbed just a bit too hard."

"Yeah. I'm beginning to get the feeling she won't be missed. Though she seemed nice enough when I ordered the cupcakes."

"Why did you order them from her anyway?" Ellie asked.

"I told you: I didn't want to tire you out."

"I know that, but why didn't you order them from Veronica?"

I shrugged. "I don't know. I stopped in for a cupcake a few weeks ago. Candy was extremely nice and the cupcake was really good. Besides, her prices are better than Veronica's. When it came time to place the order for the school I guess I figured I'd throw some money toward the new business in town.

Looking back, I probably would have saved myself a whole lot of grief if I'd just called Veronica, like I usually do."

"I wonder how much business Candy was taking from Veronica," Ellie mused.

"Every time I've driven by Candy's place she's had a line to the door," I offered. "Salinger is going to follow up on the Kevin angle, which is fine with me. He gives me the serious creeps."

"So what do we have at this point?" Zak asked. "Who are the suspects, if you can really call anyone you've spoken to a suspect?"

"Wait." Ellie hopped up and ran to her purse. She took out a small notebook. "Okay, go ahead. I'll make a list."

I sat forward before I began to recite what we knew. "Veronica was losing business, so that gives both her and her cousin, who's her partner, motive. I don't know about opportunity yet."

I took a breath before continuing. "Nick's car was towed by Candy and he was plenty mad about it, which I suppose gave him motive, but there's no way Nick would kill anyone."

"Did you ask for an alibi when you spoke to him?" Levi asked.

"No. But this is Nick. Asking for an alibi would be weird."

"I'll check with him tomorrow," Levi offered.

"Clarissa Vanderbilt lost her lease when Candy put in a better offer," I continued. "I suppose that gives her motive, along with the women who were displaced when Granny's Quilts went out of business."

Ellie wrote this bit of information down in the notebook.

"Salinger said something about a neighbor with a yappy dog, and then of course there's Willa. It seems Candy made a lot of enemies, but I'm not sure any of them had a strong enough motive to kill her. I guess it wouldn't hurt to check alibis."

"It seems to me that someone—one of the other shopkeepers who share the alley or a late shopper—must have seen something," Zak postulated. "Candy's shop is in the middle of a very busy section of town. Sure, there isn't much traffic in the alley, but still…. It wouldn't hurt to ask around when we're in town tomorrow for Hometown Christmas."

I smiled at my Zak. He had the best ideas.

"Speaking of Hometown Christmas," Ellie spoke up, "I had a call from the woman we hired to oversee the food vendors who told me that she'd come down with the flu that's been going around. I told her I'd fill in for her, but that leaves a hole in the Santa Village. I was supposed to help with the photo booth."

"I'll help with the photos; you take the food," I answered.

"Does Willa know what's going on?"

"No. And now that I know what happened I think it's best not to bother her when we can take care of it ourselves. What time were you supposed to be at the Santa Village?" I asked Ellie.

"Nine. It opens at ten, but you'll need time to get set up."

"I'm on it."

Ellie yawned.

"Maybe we should go," Levi suggested. "Tomorrow is going to be a long day."

Ellie looked at Levi. "Yeah. That might be a good idea." She tore the notes she had made from her notebook and handed them to me. "I'll see you tomorrow."

I hugged both of my friends before I saw them to the door.

"So are you going to cry again if I point out that we have the entire house all to ourselves?" Zak asked when I returned.

"It depends. What did you have in mind?"

Zak whispered in my ear.

"Zachary Zion Zimmerman. You really do have the best ideas."

Chapter 4

Saturday, December 17

When I woke up that morning I thought the most challenging part of my day would be to track down a killer, or maybe to prevent myself from crying whenever I thought about the eventuality of Scooter leaving Ashton Falls to live with his father. Never in a million years did I dream it would be ignoring the leering eyes of the town's male population as I handed out candy canes while wearing a teeny, tiny elf costume designed for someone half my size.

I should have known my day was in trouble when I arrived at the Santa Village to find the teenage girl who was supposed to play the elf had come down with the same flu that seemed to have infected half the town. When it was suggested that I just might be teeny tiny enough to fit into the ridiculously small costume I wanted to argue, but Willa already looked like she had been put through the ringer and I didn't want to add to her stress by flat-out denying her extremely fervent request.

Of course the costume was designed for a girl who was fourteen and not fully developed in the chest area, so when I put the costume on it made me look like a North Pole hooker.

"When do we take a break?" I asked Santa, who hadn't stopped leering at me since I arrived.

"We usually get a few minutes every hour, but the line is out the door and halfway around the building. I'm pretty sure we'll be lynched by stressed-out parents if we try to leave."

I let out a long breath. "Great. Another four hours without a bathroom break. Piece of cake."

I realized halfway through my shift that rather than being the jolly elf the kids expected I was the cranky elf who spent most of my time planning bodily harm to the whiny kids or their even-whinier parents. I wasn't sure what was wrong with me. I usually had a good attitude when things like this happened, which they tended to more often that I liked, but the only attitude I could muster today was irritation and resentment.

"Hey, Bambi," one of the fathers waved me over. "Will you tell Santa to hurry it up? We've been in this line forever."

What I wanted to say was *bite me*, but what I actually said was, "My name is Zoe and not Bambi. I'm sorry for the long wait, but it seems the entire population of kids between the ages of three and ten decided to show up today. If you no longer care to wait you're welcome to come back tomorrow. Or even next week. I'm sure the lines won't be so bad during the week."

Somehow I managed to get through the entire shift and was preparing to change back into my street clothes when I was informed that several of the elves who were supposed to be part of the Hometown Christmas parade had also come down with the flu and my help would be needed for just a couple more hours.

By the time I was finally relieved from elf duty the sun had already begun to set. I had no idea where Zak had ended up. The minute we'd arrived in town he'd been enlisted to help with other events that were short volunteers due to the flu.

Deciding that what I really needed was a good stiff drink, I headed toward the pub only to be waylaid by a phone call from Salinger, who insisted we needed to talk and it couldn't wait.

"So what's so important that you interrupted my intention to spend the next hour sitting alone in the bar crying in my drink?" I asked as I sat down in front of his desk.

Salinger gave me the oddest look.

"Kidding. Sort of. What can I do for you?"

"I wanted to bring you up-to-date on the Candy Kane murder investigation. I know you said you might not be up for becoming involved in this one, but I really could use your help."

I took a deep breath and sat back. "What do you have?"

"In the morning I had several admittedly weak suspects on my list. I spent most of the day tracking them down. Veronica of Veronica's Bakery was working at her own place down the street on Thursday night when Ms. Kane was murdered. I found several customers who were able to verify that. Her cousin and half owner of Veronica's Bakery, Kevin Martucci, reported that he was having dinner in Bryton Lake with some customers at the time. I verified that as well."

"Okay, so both Veronica and Kevin are off the list. How about the neighbor with the yappy dog? Did you speak to her?"

"I did. She was home alone at the time of the murder, but she said she spoke to a friend on her home phone on the night in question. The friend has confirmed it and phone records show that someone from her landline did indeed speak to the friend used as an alibi."

Dang. Our suspects were dropping like flies.

"What about Clarissa Vanderbilt?"

"Out of town and has receipts to prove it."

"Customers of Clarissa's who were displaced when the store shut down?"

"Weak motive and too many to identify and interview without additional information."

"So what you're saying is that we have nothing."

"That's exactly what I'm saying. Any ideas?"

I bit my lip as I thought about it. A woman had been murdered in a shop on Main Street where hundreds of shoppers had been mingling at the time. Someone must have seen something. It seemed we just weren't asking the right questions. Or maybe we weren't asking the right people.

"I need to do a bit of shopping anyway. How about if I casually make the rounds and ask the merchants closest to Candy Kane's Bakeshop if they saw or heard anything?"

"Would you like me to help?"

"No; people will be more apt to talk to me. Did you ever look over the receipts I found on the night of the murder?"

Salinger shook his head. "Not yet."

"It seems it would be worth our while to have a conversation with the customers who were in the bakery later in the day. Why don't you see if you can identify those people and I'll make the rounds in town?"

Salinger just grunted.

"Are you okay?" I asked.

Salinger never had been the best investigator in the world, but he really seemed off his game with this murder, and he looked like he hadn't slept in days.

"I'm fine. I haven't been sleeping well. I'll go through the receipts and then give you a call."

I headed out on foot through the festively decorated town. Candy Kane's Bakeshop was three blocks from Salinger's office and I wanted to start off with those businesses closest to the bakery, so I resisted the welcoming windows all the merchants along Main had set up as I headed toward my destination. Alex loved looking at the windows and following the unfolding story they told if you viewed them in order almost as much as I did. Maybe the two of us could come into town one evening this week to look at the decorations and have dinner.

Candy Cane's Bakeshop was situated between a clothing boutique and a T-shirt shop. Both had been open at the time Levi and I had found Candy's body, so I decided to start with those shops and then work my way west. I entered the T-shirt shop first. There were several touristy-type shops in town that sold hats and clothing with *Ashton Falls* stamped on the front.

"Can I help you?" a young male clerk who looked to be maybe twenty asked.

"Hi. My name is Zoe. Were you working on Thursday?"

"Two to ten is my regular shift. Did we speak? Am I holding something for you?"

"No. I wasn't in. I was hoping we could chat for a few minutes about the bakery next door."

"I heard it was closed. Maybe permanently. The broad who owned it got whacked."

"Yes, I heard that. She was murdered on Thursday evening. I was hoping you might have heard or seen something."

"You with the sheriff's office?"

"No. Just a friend."

The kid shrugged. "It's always pretty busy between five and eight. Especially with Christmas just around the corner. I didn't know anything was going on, so I didn't pay particular attention to the place. It was odd that it closed so early that night, though. I do remember wondering what was up with that."

"Do you know what time the shop closed?"

The kid got a distant look on his face. "I'm not sure. I remember a customer came in and asked how late the bakery was open. I told the lady I thought they were open until eight. She said the store was dark and it looked like they were closed for the day. I guess that might have been around six-thirty or six forty-five. I don't remember exactly. Like I said, it was busy and I had the music turned up. I probably wouldn't have heard it if a cannon went off."

"Do you remember seeing anyone lurking around outside?"

"Lots of folks were walking around looking at the lights."

The kid had a point. It was very noisy in the store and there were all sorts of people out walking around looking at the decorations.

"Did you know the woman who owned the bakery?"

"Not really. I might have nodded to her a time or two if we happened to cross paths dumping the trash or locking up."

"Locking up? You said you work until ten and the bakery closed at eight."

"The lady who owned the place used to stay late. I guess she might have had baking to do. I know she came in early as well. I remember thinking I would never want to own a business where you had to work so many hours. Although she seemed to have friends who stopped by to chat with her in the evenings, so I guess it wasn't so bad."

"Friends? What friends?"

The kid shrugged. "You know… old people like she was."

Candy wasn't exactly old. If I had to guess she was most likely in her midforties. "Did you notice anyone specifically?"

The kid closed one eye and screwed up his face. "I didn't pay that much attention, but there was one guy who came by pretty often. His name's Jerry. I don't know his last name. He works over at the Mexican restaurant down the street. The one with the little burro in the front window. I saw him come by with food at least a couple of times a week."

I grabbed a flyer that was on the counter and jotted down my name and cell number. "If you think of anything else will you call me?"

"Sure, I guess."

The Mexican restaurant the clerk had referred to was a block down the street, so I decided to head over to the boutique on the other side of Candy Kane's

Bakery first. The shop was elegant, sophisticated, and expensive, which meant it was absent the throngs of people and the loud music found in the T-shirt shop. There was a single clerk tidying up when I walked in the front door.

"Happy holiday." The woman smiled. "What can I help you find?"

I was about to jump right into my spiel about the bakery next door when I noticed the shop carried a small supply of maternity garments. Maybe as long as I was there I'd look for something for Ellie. A soft cashmere sweater had caught my eye the moment I walked in.

"I'm looking for a gift for my friend," I began. "She's about your height and size, but she's five months pregnant. Do the maternity tops run in the same sizes as regular ones?"

The woman pulled out a beautiful silk blouse. "They do. The tops are cut fuller to accommodate a baby bump, but if your friend wears, say, an eight when she isn't pregnant she'll wear an eight in maternity wear as well."

I picked up the sweater and held it up to the mirror. "I noticed the bakery next door is dark."

"Yes. I'm afraid the woman who owned it has passed away. I don't expect it to reopen any time soon."

"I heard she was murdered. How frightening to have it take place right next door."

"If you're interested in that sweater I have a lovely scarf that matches it perfectly."

I looked at the woman. "I'd like to see it, if you don't mind."

She opened a drawer and took out a scarf that really did blend well with the sweater.

"It's lovely." I held the scarf up to the sweater. "How late are you open?"

"We close at eight on weekdays, but we're open until nine on Saturdays."

I held the sweater up again. "I'm just not sure. I like it, but maybe I should look around some more. Can you hold it?"

"For forty-eight hours."

"I won't be able to make it in tomorrow and I'm not sure I can make it back before you close on Monday."

"I only work Friday through Sunday. We have a new girl, Betty, who works Monday through Thursday. If you want to buy the set, you can call her on Monday and work it out to come in to pick it up."

I looked at the price tag on the sweater. The dang thing cost more than my car. Well, not really. But it was the most expensive sweater I'd ever seen. Still, it was so soft and cozy. I bet Ellie would love it. And coming back for it would give me a chance to speak to the woman who was working on the night Candy was killed.

"Okay. If you'll hold it for me, I'll probably come back to pick it up on Monday." I picked up a business card from the table. "If you could just leave a note for Betty letting her know I'll contact her on Monday that would be great."

The boutique might not be loud like the T-shirt shop, but it was on the warm side, so it felt good to step out into the cool air. There were snow flurries in the air and the sky had darkened since I'd started my journey of discovery. I texted Zak, who informed me that he'd be held up for at least another hour, so I continued down the street after promising to meet him for dinner when he was finished for the day.

I was about to enter the sporting goods store next door to the boutique when my phone rang. It was Alex.

"Hey, Alex. Are you still with Ethan and Phyllis?"

"Yes. We've collected so many toys for needy kids this year. Even more than last time."

"I'm so glad. It's a good thing you and Eve are doing."

Eve Lambert was one of the three girls who lived with Phyllis, and one of Alex's best friends.

"You can still help us with the delivery next week?"

"It's on my calendar. I really had a lot of fun playing Santa with you last year. Are you finished for the day? Do you need me to come pick you up?"

"Actually, that's why I called. Eve and I want to start wrapping some of this stuff tonight. Phyllis said it was okay if I stayed over again if it's okay with you."

I wanted to say no, it wasn't okay, but instead I assured Alex that whatever she wanted to do was perfectly fine with me. Alex didn't have her house key and wanted to pick some stuff up for her overnight stay, so we arranged for Phyllis to swing by my car to pick up a spare key from me, when they were ready to head home. Alex said she'd text to get my location.

After the call I continued down the street. No one claimed to have seen or heard anything in the sporting goods store, so I headed toward the Mexican restaurant to look for Jerry. If he'd spent time with Candy on a regular basis maybe he knew something that could help make sense of her death. Of course the robbery angle was still viable; maybe there was nothing to make sense of at all.

When I arrived at the restaurant it was packed. I realized that even if Jerry was working that evening he wouldn't be able to take time away from his customers to talk to me. I decided it might still be worth it to make first contact, though, so I went up to the hostess podium and asked to speak to Jerry.

"You a friend of his?"

"Yes," I lied.

"He's in the kitchen, but don't stay long. The boss doesn't like it when friends stop by."

"I'll only be a minute," I promised.

I headed toward the kitchen and called Jerry's name when I entered through the double door.

"Yeah?" a man washing dishes asked.

"Are you Jerry?"

"What of it?"

"I wanted to speak to you about Candy Kane's murder. I can see you're busy."

Jerry tossed me a towel. "If you dry the glasses I'll talk."

Seemed fair enough. I picked up the first glass and began to rub it dry.

"Be sure to get all the spots. The boss has a coronary if there are spots."

"Got it. No spots."

Jerry went back to scraping plates and loading them into the industrial-sized dishwasher while I dried the glasses.

"I understand that you and Candy were friends," I began.

"Used to be."

"Used to be?" I asked.

"We used to live in the same town. Pretty much lost touch until she showed up here in my own backyard. What are the odds?"

Yes, I wondered what the odds were myself.

"And where are you both from exactly?"

"Small town up north. Who did you say you were again?"

"Zoe. Zoe Donovan."

"You a cop?"

"No. More of a consultant. So where exactly up north?"

The man stopped what he was doing, turned, and looked at me. "Does it really matter?"

I shrugged. "It might. Someone bludgeoned her to death. I'm just trying to figure out who might have wanted her out of the picture."

"Ain't no one from the old neighborhood. No one but me even knew she was here, and I didn't do it."

"Candy Kane is a unique sort of name. Maybe someone from your old hometown saw the shop and put two and two together."

The man snorted. "Not likely. Look, I got work to do. If that's all I can get back to it."

The closed expression on the man's face left no doubt in my mind that he was done talking. I thanked him and left.

Alex texted me just as I walked out of the restaurant. I arranged to meet her and Phyllis at my car, which was just two blocks away. I always kept an extra house key with me.

"Thanks," Alex said as I handed her the key through the passenger window.

"Out doing some shopping?" Phyllis asked.

"More like sleuthing, but I'm about done for the day. I think I'll go look for Zak."

"Speaking of sleuthing I thought of something that may turn out to be helpful."

"Oh? What is it?"

"Shortly after she moved to Ashton Falls and set up shop, I overheard one of the women who plays bingo at the senior center saying Candy wasn't who she pretended to be."

I frowned. "What do you think she meant by that?"

"I'm not sure. The woman claimed Candy Kane wasn't her real name." Phyllis paused. It appeared she was trying to think. "I wish I could remember what else she said, but I really wasn't listening."

"Do you remember who you overheard?"

"Gabriella Martini. I'm almost sure it was Gabriella Martini."

I didn't know Gabriella well, but I knew where she lived.

"Thanks for the tip. I might just pop over to say hi."

Chapter 5

I called Zak to tell him I had one more stop to make. He admitted things on his end were taking longer than expected as well, so we decided to just pick up takeout and meet at home. I promised to text when I was done.

Gabriella Martini lived in the middle of town in a neighborhood where the majority of the residents were senior citizens. As I parked in front of her small but neatly landscaped house, I wondered if I should have called before coming over. It wasn't like we were the sort of friends who might drop in on each other. No, we were definitely in more of a call-ahead type of relationship.

I didn't know her number and I was already there, so I got out of my car and headed through the snow up to her front door. I took a minute to appreciate her outdoor holiday display as I knocked on the door and waited.

"Zoe. How nice to see you," Gabriella greeted me.

"I'm sorry to just drop by, but I wanted to ask you a few questions and I was in the neighborhood."

Gabriella opened the door wider and took a step back. "Do come in. Can I get you something? Coffee? Hot cocoa?"

I entered the nicely furnished home after making sure I'd stomped all the snow off my boots. "No, I'm fine, thank you. I'll only take up a few minutes of your time."

"Come into the living room and have a seat."

The room was small but very festively decorated. There was a garland with red berries strung along the mantel that held a variety of red and white candles of varying sizes. I saw a small tree in the corner, opposite the real wood fire in the fireplace.

"What can I do for you?" Gabriella asked once I was seated.

"I'm not sure if you've heard, but there was a murder in Ashton Falls."

"A murder?" The woman paled. "I hadn't heard. I was visiting my daughter and just got back this afternoon. Who died?"

"Candy Kane, the owner of the new bakery in town."

Gabriella's lips tightened. "I see. Do they know who did it?"

"Not yet. I was chatting with Phyllis King and she mentioned she thought you knew something about Candy's background."

Gabriella settled back into the high-backed chair in which she was sitting. "Yes. I knew her before she was Candy Kane. We grew up in the same town."

What were the odds that Gabriella, Jerry, and Candy would all grow up in the same small town and wind up in Ashton Falls?

"So you must know Jerry. I forget his last name, but he works at the Mexican restaurant. He told me he grew up in the same town as Candy."

"Jerry is younger than Candy and me. I moved away a long time ago and I suspect Candy met Jerry after that."

"How long ago did you leave?"

"Must be twenty years."

"And you haven't been back in those twenty years?"

"Once. I went home to visit my mama before she passed, God bless her soul, and ran into Candy. We hadn't seen each other for years; still, I recognized her right away. She worked at a diner in town, and during my stay with Mama, I'd go in and have a bite and chat with Candy. She was married to a monster of a man at the time and I was a good listener, so Candy opened up to me despite the fact that we hadn't seen each other in years."

"She told you that her husband beat her?"

She nodded. "If what Candy told me was true, he not only beat her but abused her emotionally. During our chats I tried to talk her into leaving him, but she refused. She was terrified to do so and tried to convince me it was best if she stayed. I had my own problems to deal with and never really gave it another thought after I left town."

"And then? Did you hear from her after you returned home?"

"No. But about three years after that visit I happened across an obituary from my hometown newspaper for Donny Davenport, the man I knew to be Candy's husband. I did some checking and found an article that said it appeared he had been slowly poisoned to death. Of course Candy was a suspect, but they never found any proof to arrest her. I'm not sure where she went after that, but I do know she left town. I never saw or heard from her again until she showed up here a few months ago."

"Davenport?"

"Candy's name was Candy Conner when we were kids, which she changed to Candy Davenport when she married Donny. She must have changed her name to Candy Kane after her husband died. I don't know why. It seems like a silly name, even if you do own a bakeshop."

"Yes, I guess it does. Did Candy know you lived here?"

Gabriella paused. "No. I don't think it ever came up during the course of our conversations."

"Did you renew your relationship after she moved to Ashton Falls?"

"No. She knew I knew who she really was. She asked me to keep her secret and I didn't feel comfortable with the lie, so I decided to avoid her altogether."

I adjusted my position slightly so that I was looking more directly at Gabriella.

"Do you know why she chose to move here?"

"I have no idea. I guess she needed a place to start over yet again and picked here."

"Do you know of anyone Candy was close enough to that she might have kept in touch with during the years after she left her hometown and showed up here?"

"She had a sister. I don't know if she's even still alive. She left the small town where we grew up the minute she turned eighteen. Her name was Janell."

I asked Gabriella to let me know if she thought of anything else and then thanked her and headed home for dinner with Zak.

I called Salinger and filled him in while I walked the dogs, who acted like they had been left alone for a century and not just a single day. Salinger promised to follow up to see what he could learn about not only

Candy and her sister Janell but also Jerry from the Mexican restaurant.

Then I willed myself to relax. It was a beautiful night and I had done what I could. It had started to snow again, but the wind we'd had earlier had gone, so the gentle flakes seemed to float on the air, drifting to and fro as they made their way toward the surface of the lake. Charlie, Bella, and Digger were all excited to have a chance to run, so they went back and forth along the snow-covered beach as I followed slowly wearing my snowshoes.

I couldn't help but wonder how Scooter was doing. I knew Alex would be having a fantastic time with Phyllis and the three girls who lived with her, but I worried about Scooter alone with a father he was estranged from and an almost stepmom-to-be he'd just met. He had his own cell phone and I was tempted to call him, but Zak and I had agreed not to interfere in his visit with his father in any way. If Scooter needed me, he could text me, and the fact that he hadn't should indicate he was fine. Still, I worried.

I tucked my red-mittened hands up under my arms against the chill in the air. It had been a while since I'd enjoyed a solitary walk on the beach after dark. The property on which Zak and I lived was located on an isolated part of the beach, with only Ellie and the boathouse to the left and my parents' house farther down the beach to the right. I rarely cross paths with anyone while out walking, but tonight I'd almost welcome the distraction of a passerby to take me away from my thoughts.

"You guys ready to head back?" I asked the dogs.

Charlie came running at the sound of my voice and the others followed suit. I turned around and used the flashlight I carried to light the way.

By the time I returned home Zak's truck was in the driveway.

"Something smells good," I said after I'd taken off my snowshoes, stomped the snow from my boots, and entered the house through the mudroom off the kitchen.

"Stir-fry. I was going to pick up takeout as we discussed, but then it occurred to me that a stir-fry would be just as easy, would be healthier, and would taste better. I opened a bottle of wine if you want a glass."

"Maybe with dinner. I'm going to run up and change out of these wet clothes."

"You have ten minutes."

"I'll hurry."

I could hear Zak getting the dogs their dinner as I made my way through the living area, which Zak had decorated from top to bottom. It felt like a Christmas fairyland when the overhead lights were out and there were only the lights from the tree and the fireplace to provide a warm glow. Zak had decorated the mantel with garlands and candles, and the banister had strings of evergreens wound around it.

In the bedroom I quickly took off my damp clothes and changed into warm sweats. The lights in the bedroom, like the rest of the house, lent an air of romance to the evening. Maybe a kid-free weekend wouldn't be so bad after all.

"This is ready if you want to grab a couple of plates," Zak called.

I poured the wine while Zak spooned stir-fry onto the plates. We decided to eat in the living room, where the tree and the fire provided a romantic setting.

"So, how did your day go?" Zak asked.

Enough time had passed that I could find humor in my embarrassing stint as a North Pole hooker elf. Once I'd exhausted that subject Zak filled me in on his pretty awful day. It seemed elves weren't the only ones coming down with the flu. Zak had spent his day filling in for a variety of people who had called in sick.

"I hate to think what we might be walking into tomorrow," I said as I sipped my wine.

"Maybe we should call in sick like everyone else," Zak teased.

"I wish."

"If you end up with elf duty again call me. I'm sorry I missed it."

I shot Zak a dirty look.

"I guess we should expect that tomorrow will be as hectic as today and plan to get an early start," Zak suggested.

I yawned. "Yeah. I guess."

"You look exhausted. Why don't you go up and I'll take care of the dishes?"

I was tempted to take Zak up on his offer, but he looked as tired as I did. "We'll do them together. It won't take long."

Christmas music played softly in the background as Zak and I worked together to put the kitchen in order. It really was kind of nice. After Alex and Scooter had moved in with us full-time there hadn't been a lot of nights when it was just the two of us, enjoying the warmth of the house as we worked side by side. Not that I'd trade Scooter and Alex for any amount of alone time. I just realized that maybe I should try harder to enjoy the time we had.

"Who could that be?" I asked as the house phone rang.

"I don't know. I'll get it."

My heart began to pound as I watched the color drain from Zak's face. I couldn't make out exactly what was going on, but I knew it wasn't good.

"What is it?' I asked after Zak hung up.

"That was Scooter's dad."

"What's wrong with Scooter?" I felt the panic begin to build.

"He's gone."

"Gone?" I squeaked in a small voice that barely made a sound.

"Apparently, Scooter's dad and his fiancée wanted to go to dinner, but Scooter didn't, so they left him in the motel room. When they got back he was gone. He called to see if he was here."

"It's freezing outside. We have to find him."

Zak was already pulling on his coat. "You stay here in case he calls or comes home. I'll go look for him."

"Tucker," I said, mentioning the name of Scooter's best friend. "I bet he went to Tucker's."

I picked up the phone and called Tucker's house, but there was no answer. I left a message.

"He has his phone," I realized. I called the number, but it went straight to voice mail. I left a nearly hysterical message begging him to call us.

"I'm going to check the arcade and a few of the other places he likes to go. Call Alex. Maybe she's heard from him. And maybe your parents. Scooter might go there if he wanted to hide out. Call me if you find him."

With that, Zak was out the door.

After a very stressful couple of hours of searching we found Scooter hiding in my parents' pool house.

"You scared me to death," I sobbed as I hugged the twelve-year-old boy with all my might.

"I'm sorry. I didn't mean to worry you."

"Why did you run away?"

"I heard my dad talking about moving all of us to Los Angeles. I don't want to move there. I don't want to move anywhere. I like living here with you and Zak and Alex."

I glanced at Zak, who stood next to us. We'd agreed not to interfere with Scooter's relationship with his father, but it was clear Scooter wanted to stay in Ashton Falls.

Scooter looked up at Zak. "Please don't make me go."

Zak opened his arms and Scooter ran into them. "I can't make any promises, but I'll talk to your dad. In the meantime, you need to promise not to run away again. Something could have happened to you."

"I knew my way here."

"It's snowing," I said as Scooter clung to Zak.

"We'd better call Scooter's dad," Zak said. "He's probably worried sick."

"I'll do it. My parents are waiting in the house. I'll fill them in as well."

When I'd called my parents while we were looking, my dad had offered to help us. After all of Scooter's favorite places had been searched my dad had thought of checking the pool house. It was a good thing he had; if not, it would have been a very long night of worry about the boy who meant so much to all of us.

"How is he?" my mom asked. Although they weren't in any way related, I knew my parents thought of Alex and Scooter as their grandchildren.

"He's fine. He doesn't want to go back to the motel. I'm going to call Scooter's dad to ask him to let Scooter stay with us tonight. I hope he agrees because there isn't anything we can do to make him agree if he doesn't."

"Zak never pursued any sort of a formal guardianship designation?" my dad asked.

"No. It's all been very informal. Scooter's dad didn't want him and we did, so everyone was happy. Now? Now I don't know what's going to happen."

My mom hugged me. It really sucked when you felt so helpless in a situation that was so very important.

Chapter 6

Sunday, December 18

As it turned out, his dad was fine with us taking Scooter home last night. He didn't make any sort of a commitment one way or the other beyond that, but he did agree to meet with Zak to discuss the situation this morning. Zak thought it best if he went alone, so I found myself on pins and needles while I waited. I don't know what I was going to do if Scooter's dad carried out his plan to move his family to Los Angeles. Nothing, I suppose. I mean really, what could we do?

"Has there been any word?" Ellie asked as she walked in through the kitchen door with her dog Shep and Levi's dog Karloff on her heels. I had of course called her the previous evening when we were looking for Scooter, and then again after we'd found him, so she knew what was going on.

"Not yet. I hate this waiting. I should have insisted on going with Zak."

"I think maybe Zak was right about going alone. He can talk to Scooter's dad man to man."

"Maybe. Coffee?"

"Caffeine…" Ellie said, reminding me that she was staying away from the stuff while pregnant.

"Hot cocoa?"

"I'd love some."

I got up from the barstool I was sitting on to heat the milk.

"Where's Scooter?" Ellie asked.

"Sleeping. He was pretty worn out. Plus, I don't think he slept very well while he was away. I think he's pretty scared Zak won't be able to work out a deal with his dad and he'll have to move away."

"He hasn't always been the best dad, but I don't think he'd force the move now that he knows how important it is to Scooter to stay."

I handed Ellie her hot cocoa. "I hope so." I looked around the festively decorated kitchen and felt hollow inside. What good were decorations to brighten your environment if you couldn't be with the ones you loved?

"Did Levi head over to Hometown Christmas?" I wondered.

"Yeah. As expected, we're short bodies again today. I'm going to head over as well in a little while, but I wanted to stop by to see how you were doing before volunteer duty swallowed me whole for the day. I know how hard this is."

I realized Ellie did know exactly what I was feeling. She'd fallen in love with a child once, only to have her removed from her life when her father decided he was going to move back to his hometown and renew his relationship with the child's mother. Everyone, including Ellie, had agreed it was probably the best thing for the child, but that didn't ease Ellie's pain when the toddler she had grown to love was ripped from her life.

"I told Willa that you and Zak might not make it today," Ellie added.

"We'll wait to see what happens," I answered noncommittally. "If Zak gets everything settled and Scooter is able to stay, I'll drop him off at Tucker's and come by to do what I can. I know how much this means to the town."

"I think poor Willa is about to implode. You know how important this event is to her, and then add on the fact that everyone is sick *and* Salinger is still hounding her about her behavior on the night Candy died and you have a meltdown waiting to happen."

I thought about what Ellie had just said. Salinger had spoken to Willa, who'd claimed to have gone home after she left the bakery on Thursday night. She lived alone, so she didn't have an alibi, which admittedly complicated things. "I have to agree that Willa's behavior was odd that night, but I'm kind of surprised Salinger is pursuing her as a viable suspect. He has to know she wouldn't kill anyone."

Ellie paused before answering, a thoughtful expression on her face. "Willa is a good woman with a good heart, but she can also be hotheaded. I've thought about this quite a bit, actually. If Candy was rude or argumentative, if she challenged Willa's authority to enforce the regulation she was there to enforce, I can kind of see her flipping out. Maybe she grabbed the rolling pin and hit her before she even knew what she was doing."

"Yeah, but we all agreed she wouldn't just leave if that had happened."

"True, but maybe she didn't have time to think about it. Maybe she panicked and ran, and by the time she had a chance to catch her breath and make a decision about doing the right thing you had already found the body. Salinger did say the murder had occurred just a short time before you arrived."

Ellie had a good point. A very good point. It could very well have gone down that way. I just hoped it hadn't.

I was a nervous wreck by the time Zak got home.

"Well?" I demanded before he even had a chance to take off his jacket.

"Is Scooter up?"

"He hasn't come down yet."

Zak hung his jacket on the coatrack and poured himself a cup of coffee.

"What happened?" I asked again. "What did Scooter's dad say when you told him that you thought it would be best to let Scooter stay here with us?"

"He said he'd think about it."

"That's it? You've been gone for two hours and all he said was that he'd think about it?"

Zak ran his hand through his hair. I could see he was both stressed and fatigued. "We talked about a lot of things. How well Scooter is doing in school and the fact that if he moved him now he'd have to start over in a new school midyear. We talked about the fact that Scooter has friends he can depend on and that he's a member of several sporting teams, which provides him with a sense of self-worth and community. We talked about Alex and how she's like a sister to Scooter. Like I said, we talked about a lot of things."

I was pretty sure I was going to cry. Zak didn't look at all like his usual confident self.

"That wasn't enough?" I said in a tiny voice.

"I don't know. He seemed to listen to what I was saying and he acknowledged that everything I said was important. He admitted that he'd been a mess when he left Scooter with us and that our participation in his life has made all the difference. He also said he'd changed. He's a new man. He quit drinking, he has a new fiancée and a new job. He worked hard and got his life back on track and he wants another chance with his son."

Tears streamed down my face. "Do you think he's going to take him against his will?"

"I don't know. I have to admit I feel for the man. If Scooter was my son and I had a second chance to be a father I'd take it." Zak looked at me. He caressed the side of my cheek with his finger and looked me directly in the eye. "Scooter doesn't belong to us. He isn't our son. I believe Scooter's father is sincere in his desire to finally be the dad Scooter deserves. It will kill me if Scooter leaves, but I don't see how we can get between a father and his child."

"But Scooter doesn't want to go."

"Scooter's scared. He doesn't want to leave everything he finds comfortable. I understand that, but I also think he may regret it in the long run if he doesn't try to reconnect with his dad now. It's unfortunate Scooter's dad's new job is so far away. It would be easier on Scooter if his dad was coming back to Ashton Falls and he didn't have to move in order to reestablish a relationship with the man who had at one point been an important person in his life."

I supposed Zak was right. Scooter's dad was a good father and a good man until his wife died and he'd dealt with his grief by diving into a whiskey bottle. "Can't we get him a job? Here? Can't we find him a job here so Scooter can stay *and* get to know his dad again?"

Zak took a deep breath. "Doing what?"

I frowned. "I don't know. What does Scooter's dad do?"

"His new job is in manufacturing. He didn't go into any sort of detail about it when we spoke."

"Okay, so we don't have a factory," I admitted. "But there has to be something."

Zak hugged me so tight I almost couldn't breathe. I melted into his body as he took comfort in mine.

"I'm not sure what the right thing to do is," Zak whispered in my ear.

I pulled back slightly. "What do you mean?"

"We're talking about manipulating a man's life to suit our own needs. What if finding him a job to keep Scooter close isn't what's right for him?"

I hadn't thought of that.

Zak wiped a tear from my cheek with his finger. "We need to make whatever's going to happen as easy as we can for Scooter. If it turns out he has to move we need to support that so Scooter knows it's the right thing for him. If we act scared—if we put up resistance—he will too, and that will just make the whole thing much harder."

"Okay," I whispered.

"Even if it means he has to leave."

I nodded. I wanted to agree, but I couldn't speak.

Zak talked to Scooter when he got up and somehow managed to convince him to spend the day with his dad as long as he was allowed to bring his best friend, Tucker, along, and as long as he was allowed to come back to our house at the end of the day. Somehow Zak also managed to convince Scooter's father to take things slowly. To get to know his son again on Scooter's timetable rather than his own. I really did hope Scooter had a good day with his dad, even if I was terrified about what a good day today might mean in the long run.

When we arrived at Hometown Christmas, Zak was whisked away to help with setting up the community center for the spaghetti dinner that was being held that night and I was once again stuck in the Santa Village. Normally I enjoyed Hometown Christmas, but this year Santa couldn't pull up stakes and return to the North Pole soon enough as far as I was concerned.

I was halfway through my shift as an elf when Ellie came to find me. I wanted to hug her when she announced that I was needed elsewhere and they'd arranged for the teenage daughter of one of the other volunteers to finish my shift for me.

"Thank you, thank you." I hugged Ellie as I headed to the changing room.

"Don't thank me just yet."

I paused and looked at my best friend. "You have something even worse you need me to do?"

"No. It's not that. It's Willa. Some guy in a black suit who identified himself as state police came by and picked her up."

"State police? Was Salinger with him?"

"No. The guy was alone. The last thing Willa said as she was being helped into the man's car was *get Zoe*, so here I am, getting Zoe."

"Okay. Give me a minute to change and I'll see what I can find out."

Salinger wasn't in his office when I stopped by there, nor was he answering his phone. The woman who was working at the reception desk told me that he'd left with some men from the state and she didn't know when he might return or how to get hold of him. If I had an emergency, I should call 911 and someone would respond. I didn't have an emergency, so I ignored her advice and went to find Ellie.

"Did you find out what happened?" Ellie asked as soon as I found her at the gingerbread decorating contest.

"No. Salinger isn't in and there's a temp at the front desk I've never met. I'm going to assume the state police found evidence that makes Willa an even stronger suspect."

"So what should we do? How can we help her?"

I frowned and looked around the crowded room. There were kids aged five to ninety-five making gingerbread houses, giving the room a festive feel, but all I could think about was murder and betrayal.

"I'm not sure," I finally answered. "Can you take a break so we can chat?"

Ellie looked toward the front of the room. "Yeah. Just give me a minute. I'll go tell the event chairperson that I'm not feeling well. It's amazing how much slack others are willing to cut you when you're five months pregnant."

When Ellie returned we decided to head over to Rosie's for lunch so we could discuss what to do. If Willa had been picked up by the state police she'd most likely been taken to Bryton Lake. We'd probably just have to wait until Salinger called me back before we could find out all the details of what was going on.

I ordered a tuna melt and Ellie ordered a chef's salad. Then we settled in for our discussion.

"I don't claim to have a clue about what's going on, but I have to believe the state police know something we don't if they're involved," I began.

"Yeah. I had the same thought."

"And if the state police are involved I suppose Candy's history could play into this whole thing."

"What are you talking about? What history?"

I'd forgotten I hadn't filled Ellie in after I'd spoken to Gabriella. So I told her now about the fact that Candy Kane had grown up as Candy Conner, who married a man named Davenport, and they'd lived in a small town north of Ashton Falls. "Gabriella indicated that Candy's husband died under mysterious circumstances."

"Mysterious?"

"He was slowly being poisoned to death. Candy was a suspect at the time, particularly because her husband was known to abuse her, but she denied the allegations and there was never enough evidence to arrest her. Gabriella said she'd lost touch with Candy and hadn't seen her in a very long time, but she had known she'd moved away from the town where they'd grown up after the death of her husband. She'd neither seen nor heard from her again until she'd moved to Ashton Falls a few months ago."

The conversation paused as the waitress brought over our food.

"So what does all this mean?" Ellie asked after the waitress left.

"I'm not sure, but I bet there's more going on than we think." I glanced at my phone. "I wish Salinger would call."

Ellie looked directly at me. "Do you think Willa did it? Do you think she's guilty of killing Candy?"

Did I? "No," I decided. "I don't think Willa killed Candy." I frowned. "I wonder who saw Willa leaving the bakery, though. So far not a single person I've talked to remembers hearing or seeing anything."

"Good question. I guess you'll have to ask Salinger."

"Yeah. I will."

Ellie and I settled in with our own thoughts while we ate. I tried to organize the suspects in my mind. Jerry from the Mexican restaurant had seemed nervous and fidgety when I spoke to him. If he came by on a regular basis to share dinner with Candy, could he have been there on the night she was killed, and might they have argued? I hadn't seen any takeout containers in the bakery, but he might have cleaned up afterward. I also had neglected to get his alibi for the night of the murder. Of course he hadn't been real forthcoming with any information, so I sort of doubted he'd be willing to tell me what he'd been doing on Thursday night.

"So what now?" Ellie asked after we'd mostly finished our food.

"One of the things I wanted to do was to go through the receipts Candy collected the day she died. I noticed she assigned her customers a number, and there was a book with details about each of them. I thought if we knew who was in the bakery that day it might at the very least give us a place to start. The problem is that Salinger took the book and receipts from me that first night. He said he'd go through them. The last time I spoke to him he said he hadn't gotten around to it yet."

"I agree that speaking to the customers who were in on the day of the murder could lead to a clue, but unless Salinger calls you back I don't see that there's much we can do at this point."

"Sure there is. I just need a distraction. A pregnant woman in need of assistance should do the trick."

"I want to go on record to state that I do not like this one little bit!" Ellie complained.

"It'll be a cinch. I just need you to distract the woman at the desk while I sneak past. Chances are Salinger has the receipts and notebook sitting on top of his desk. I'll grab them and be out in under a minute."

Ellie had a pained look on her face. "You're suggesting we steal evidence from the sheriff's office. I'm certain there are pretty stiff penalties for doing something like that. I don't want to have this baby in prison."

"You won't go to prison. Neither of us will. If Salinger asks, I'll just tell him I had a lead I needed to follow up on."

Ellie groaned as I pulled up in front of the county offices.

"How exactly am I supposed to distract this woman long enough for you to sneak by?"

"I don't suppose you can puke on demand?"

"No, I can't puke on demand."

"Okay, then, you'll have to settle for being dizzy. Just tell her you were walking past the office and got really dizzy. Tell her you need a glass of water. Maybe act like you think you're going to faint."

"Faint?"

I sighed. "Just use your imagination."

Ellie rolled her eyes, but she followed me down the walk to Salinger's office. She asked for a glass of water, which distracted the receptionist long enough for me to get in through the front door, head down the hall, and sneak into Salinger's office, closing the door behind me. He had actually stashed the receipts and the notebook in a desk drawer, so it took me a bit longer than I'd anticipated to retrieve them. Once I'd shoved everything into my jacket pocket I cracked open the door and peeked into the reception area. The receptionist's back was to me and I managed to make eye contact with Ellie, who was standing at the counter, sipping her water and chatting with the woman. I motioned for her to distract the receptionist again so I could sneak out.

Ellie put her hand to her head. "Wow. I really feel dizzy."

"Should I call someone for you? Maybe your husband?"

"I'm not married."

"Oh. I'm sorry. A friend?"

"No. I've been on my feet all day. Maybe I just need to sit down."

Ellie took a step away from the counter and then swayed.

"Are you okay?" The receptionist ran around the counter and grabbed Ellie's arm to help support her.

"Yeah. I'm fine. Maybe you can just help me over to that chair."

I dashed down the hall and out the door while the woman was busy helping Ellie. I waited for a minute, then came in through the front door. "Ellie. What are you doing here?"

Ellie explained about needing a drink and a chance to sit down before asking if I was there to see Salinger. I said I was, and the receptionist informed me that he wasn't in. I volunteered to drive Ellie home and we left.

"I can't believe that worked," Ellie said as we headed to the car.

"The woman didn't expect anyone to sneak in, so she wasn't looking for anyone to sneak in."

"Did you find what you were looking for?"

"Yes. Let's go back to the house to see what we can make of everything."

"Okay. Let's stop by my place first and grab Shep and Karloff."

Chapter 7

We picked up the dogs, I called Zak, and Ellie called Levi, both of us telling them what was going on. Then we took all five dogs for a walk on the beach. We still had a couple of hours of light and the path along the sand was worn down to the point where it wasn't icy, so mother hen that I seem to be of late, I wasn't too worried about Ellie taking the walk with me.

"This is nice," she said. "I haven't gotten out much lately. Levi seems to have this idea that I need to be coddled twenty-four seven. I've tried telling him that I'm not sick and I'm not made of glass, but he doesn't seem to understand that it's possible to be pregnant *and* take care of yourself."

"I think it's sweet that he wants to take care of you."

"Sweet? Really? Just wait until you're pregnant and Zak won't hardly let you take a shower by yourself."

I laughed. "Yeah, I can see that would be irritating. On the other hand, being overprotective is a lot better than most of the scenarios we both envisioned when you first found out you were having Levi's baby."

"I guess that's true. And he's started to back off a little now that I'm feeling better. I was half-expecting him to insist that I was too fragile to help out at Hometown Christmas."

I took Ellie's hand in mine and gave it a squeeze in an offer of comfort. It was nice to walk hand in hand with my best friend down the deserted beach, even if it was covered in snow.

"Not to be nosy," I said after a while, "but have you and Levi talked any more about your relationship in general?"

Ellie sighed. "No. Not really. He's practically living at the boathouse, but he sleeps on the sofa even if it is too short for him. I've pointed out on more than one occasion that he has a perfectly good bed at his apartment and I don't need to be watched constantly, but he insists he's fine and wants to be here if I should need anything. At least he's had work to go to, but now that school is out for two weeks I'm not sure if I can take him constantly being underfoot."

"There was a time you liked him being underfoot," I pointed out.

"I know. It's just that I'm trying to keep a level head about this whole thing. It's hard to remember my resolve to think with my head and not my heart when he's there all the time, being so sweet and charming."

I took several more steps before replying. "I know Levi hurt you badly and I know he said a million times he didn't want children, but it really does look as if he's changed his mind about that. He seems to be genuinely excited about the prospect of being a father. I know he loves you and I know you love him. Maybe you should let yourself have this. He wants back into your life. Maybe you should let him in."

Ellie stopped walking. She turned and looked at me. "I want that more than anything, but what if his desire to be a father wears off once he is one? Parenting isn't all about hugs and cuddles. It can be hard and exhausting as well. What if Levi isn't up for that?"

Ellie was making sense. Even I wasn't sure Levi really understood what he was getting into and how much his life would change once the baby was born.

"I get it," I finally said. "And you know I'm here for you no matter what."

"I know. That means a lot. More than you can know."

"How about we head back for some hot cocoa? I think the dogs are worn out enough."

By the time we returned to the house and got the dogs fed and settled the sun was low in the sky. It occurred to me that I really should check on both Scooter and Alex. I started by calling Zak and asking if he knew what was going on with both of the children who shared our lives. Zak reported that Phyllis was going to drop Alex off after she took all the girls to dinner, and Scooter's dad was going to drop him off after dinner. Zak thought he and Levi would be home in about an hour, so Ellie and I decided to use the time we would be waiting to go through the receipts.

"It looks like these are all time- and date-stamped," I began. "Some have customer numbers and some don't. I'm guessing Candy only kept records of the transactions of repeat customers." I thumbed through the individual slips of paper. "Here's a receipt from the morning of the murder that just shows that someone bought a dozen doughnuts. An hour later Tawny Upton came in and picked up a cake for her daughter's birthday."

I thumbed through the notebook, looking for the customer number assigned to Tawny on the receipt. Sure enough, there was a corresponding entry in the notebook, with all the purchases Tawny had made, along with a note that her son was allergic to strawberries. Tawny, who was both a friend and a member of the events committee, had picked up the cake early in the day, so I doubted she'd have much insight into Candy's death, but I made a note to speak to her anyway. You never knew when some small detail might break a case wide open.

"Who else came in that you recognize?" Ellie asked.

"Hazel bought a pie—chocolate—so I'm guessing my grandpa was coming for dinner. He loves his chocolate pie. She was in at three-thirty. Ethan was in at four and purchased a cheesecake, and Jeremy was there at five-thirty. He bought a cake. I guess we can start there. It looks like Jeremy was the last customer of the day with a customer number. There are several receipts for cookies, cupcakes, and doughnuts after that, but none have a customer number. Most look like walk-in orders."

"Do they have time stamps?"

"Yeah. Why?"

"What time was the last receipt issued?"

I looked at the order form. "Six thirty-two."

"And what time did you get there?"

"Around seven-fifteen." I looked at Ellie. "I wonder who ordered a cup of coffee and two oatmeal cookies at six forty-two, and whether they stayed to eat them or took them to go."

"Too bad there's no name."

"Yeah. Too bad."

The guys were due any minute, so Ellie decided to start dinner while I called the people on my list. Hazel confirmed that she'd bought a chocolate pie and that my grandfather had been her dinner guest. She said she hadn't seen anything odd when she was at the bakery and that Candy had seemed to be in a good mood.

Tawny had been in that morning for her daughter's birthday cake. She likewise had failed to notice anything odd and she hadn't really picked up on a vibe of any sort from Candy; the bakery was crowded with the morning crowd, so the two of them hadn't spoken.

Ethan reported that he'd been invited over to Phyllis's for dinner and had decided to pick up a cheesecake. I paused to wonder again if there was something going on between him and Phyllis. They'd been friends forever, but it really did seem they'd been spending a lot of time together lately.

I called Jeremy, my right-hand man and manager of Zoe's Zoo, the wild and domestic animal control and rehabilitation shelter I owned and operated, but he didn't pick up, so I left a message. Jeremy had recently married a woman with a daughter in elementary school, completing the family circle along with his two-year-old daughter, Morgan Rose.

"It looks like the guys are here," Ellie announced.

"Okay; let's go ahead and eat. Maybe Salinger will return my call by the time we're done, and hopefully he'll be able to shed some light on what exactly is going on."

By the time we'd finished dinner Alex and Scooter were both home. They said hi and then headed to their rooms to watch TV and, probably, gab with the friends they'd just left on their phones. Zak did the dishes while Levi took the dogs out for a quick break and Ellie and I settled in the living room in front of the tree and the crackling fire. Someone—I suspected Zak—had lit bayberry candles, giving the room a cozy feel combined with the lights and the soft Christmas jazz playing on the stereo.

"It looks like you've been busy." Ellie nodded toward the brightly wrapped gifts under the tree.

"More like Zak has been busy. We made a list for the kids together, but then Zak went online and ordered everything before I even knew what he was doing. At first I was sad I wasn't going to have the joy of standing in long lines and fighting with other harried shoppers for the last of some popular item at the mall, but with everything that's going on, I think I'm just as glad he handled things."

"I hear you. I just don't have the energy this year. I do want to get something nice for Levi, but I can't decide what. I'm afraid anything I get for him will send a message of some type. Do I get him the thanks-for-being-my-pal sweater, or the let's-get romantic silk pajamas? Of course I could play it safe and get him the you're-like-a-brother-to-me piece of sporting equipment."

I thought about Levi and the ring I knew he was still carrying around. A gift—any gift—between the two of them was definitely going to have a message, real or inferred, that went along with it.

"What are you getting for Zak?"

"I have no idea. I've spent more time agonizing over that very question than I should. I know he'll be happy with whatever I choose, but I want to get him something special. Something that shows him how much I love him, not just some generic item from a catalog or the mall."

"Christmas certainly has become stressful."

"Tell me about it," I agreed.

I heard the doorbell in the background, followed by Zak talking to someone who sounded a lot like Jeremy. When the two of them walked into the living room together I knew I'd been right.

"Hey, Jeremy. What are you doing here? Is something wrong at the Zoo?"

"No, nothing's wrong. I got your voice-mail message and decided to stop by."

"You didn't need to do that. You could have just called."

"It's not a problem. Jessica is getting the girls to bed. What's up?"

Zak offered Jeremy a beer. He accepted and sat down in one of the chairs that framed the sofa on two sides.

"I noticed you bought a cake on Thursday from Candy Kane's Bakeshop."

"I suspected you were investigating."

"Sort of, in an unofficial capacity. You were one of Candy's last customers."

"And you wondered if I'd seen a killer lurking in the shadows?"

"You didn't, did you? 'Cause that would make this investigation a whole lot easier."

"No, I didn't, but after getting your call I took a moment to think about what I did see. I figured that was probably why you called."

"And...?"

"And there *was* something odd. When I went in, Candy was sitting in one of the booths with a man I didn't recognize. They'd been talking, but they stopped as soon as I came in. Candy got up to help me, but I think now that she was nervous. She kept glancing at the man the entire time I was in the shop."

"Was he still there when you left?"

"Yes."

"Can you describe him?"

"About five ten. Maybe two hundred pounds. Red hair. Sort of long and curly. I didn't notice his eye color. He was wearing a black pullover, but he was sitting down, so I didn't notice what he had on the bottom half of his body."

"Anything else?"

"He cleared his throat. Often. Like he had eaten something that hadn't quite gone down right. There were coffee cups on the table but no plates or other evidence that they'd shared food. I guess the plates might already have been cleared away."

Well, that was something. Not a lot but something.

"Was anyone else in the bakery?"

"Not in the front, but the more I think about it, the more it seems I heard someone in the kitchen. I could be mistaken, but it occurred to me at the time that Candy might have hired an assistant with the busy holiday season and all."

An assistant. I'd never even stopped to consider that Candy might have someone working for her, but it would be hard to both bake and work the counter during the holidays, so it made sense that she would have help. I decided the next thing I needed to do was find an answer to that very question.

Levi and Ellie left not long after Jeremy, and I headed upstairs to check on the kids while Zak went to deal with some emails he needed to return.

"So how was your weekend?" I asked Alex.

"Awesome." She grinned. "We not only collected more toys for our toy drive than we did last year but Phyllis found a company willing to publish my book."

"I'm so proud of you." I hugged Alex. "That's such awesome news."

"It is. The publisher is going to help a lot with advertising and distribution. They're even giving us a larger royalty than usual because all my earnings are going to charity. When I started writing the book it was just for me; something fun to do on a snowy day. But now that I know that lots and lots of people are going to be reading it, I'm kind of nervous."

"Nervous?"

"What if it isn't good?"

"I'm sure it's good. Phyllis wouldn't be helping you to publish it if it wasn't. Can I read it?"

"Not yet. I'll be too scared that you won't like it."

"I'm sure I will."

"I know you'll say you like it even if you don't, so knowing that makes me even more nervous. You can read it when it's published, like everyone else."

"And when will it be published?"

"Next year in time for Christmas." Alex placed her hands over her heart and smiled. "Phyllis said something about September."

I hugged Alex again. "I'm sure Charlie will be thrilled that the story of him on the Candy Cane Express will be used to help kids who are less fortunate. Are we still on for the wrapping party for this year's gifts on Thursday?"

She nodded. "I have a lot of people coming over to help."

When I left Alex's room I headed to Scooter's. Unlike Alex, who was bouncing off the wall with happiness, Scooter looked withdrawn and thoughtful.

I sat down on the edge of his bed and put my arm around him. "Something on your mind?"

He just shrugged.

"Did you have a nice day with your dad?"

Another shrug.

"You know you can talk to me. You can tell me anything."

"I know."

"You have a lot to think about, but if you want to talk you can come to Zak or me anytime. No matter what."

"'Kay."

I got up and began to straighten up the room. "Did you and Tucker go to the Santa Village today? I didn't see you, but I left early."

"Santa is for babies. We went to the sledding hill."

"That sounds like fun. Now that the resorts are open we'll have to go skiing. Maybe after Christmas."

A tear slid down Scooter's cheek. *Good going, Zoe; you made the kid cry.*

I stopped what I was doing and sat back down next to him. "Do you want to tell me about it?"

"It's just that I don't know what's going to happen. I don't even know if I'll be here to go skiing after Christmas. I'm scared. I tried to ask my dad, but he just said he had some things to think over. It's not fair, you know?"

"I know."

"I'm old enough to make my own decisions."

"I know."

"I love my dad, but I don't want to move."

"I know."

"I won't have any friends and I won't be able to play Little League with Tucker. We're going to have the most awesome team ever this year."

I didn't respond.

Scooter was quiet for a minute. Eventually, he said, "It seems like Dad is doing better. Do you think he's doing better?"

"I do."

"He was so sad when Mom died, but now he has Brandy. He says it will be like old times. That we'll have fun like we used to. That things will be totally awesome, just like they used to be. Do you think that's true?"

I took a deep breath and took Scooter's hand in mine. "I don't know if it's ever possible for things to go back to being exactly the way they were. You've changed. Your dad has changed. Brandy seems awesome, but she isn't your mom. Still, I do think that if your dad is better and wants to have a life with you, maybe the two of you can find a new kind of awesome. I know moving will be hard, but maybe finding a new kind of awesome with your dad could be worth it."

Scooter put his head in my lap and sobbed. I struggled not to join him, but I knew I had to be strong for him. Zak was right; as hard as this was for us, if it was possible for Scooter to have a life with his dad, who were we not to support that?

"If I have to move can I come back to visit?"

"Absolutely. As often as you want. I want you to know that whatever happens we'll always have an open door and a warm bed for you. We love you and we'll always be here for you."

Chapter 8

Thursday December 22

It had been a long and frustrating week. Scooter's dad was still in town and Scooter continued to spend every day with him, although he'd been allowed to come home every night. I had the sense that he and his dad were getting along a little better, and Scooter definitely wasn't as angsty as he had been, but I was still worried. Zak had spoken to Scooter's father on several occasions and reported back that he planned to remain in Ashton Falls until after Christmas, and that he'd decided not to make a definite decision about Scooter's fate until after Christmas as well.

On one hand, I was glad he was taking the time to really think things through, and if in the end he decided to insist that Scooter leave with him, I was glad he was waiting until after Christmas to make his announcement. On the other hand, the not knowing was tough on Scooter. Heck, it was tough on everyone. Anytime the subject of the conversation navigated toward an event in the future there was an awkward and painful silence when we realized Scooter might not be here to share it with us.

Zak had invited Scooter's dad and his fiancée to spend Christmas with us and while he had yet to commit, it seemed as if he was warming up to the idea. Still, I wouldn't be at all surprised if he decided not to join us. I was trying to keep an open mind about the situation, but if I was totally honest, I wasn't completely convinced he'd made a permanent change to the good. Yes, he seemed to be trying, and yes, he most definitely was a better man than the one who'd abandoned Scooter more than two years ago, but Scooter had mentioned that his father hadn't actually started his new job yet and that he'd only just met his fiancée three months ago.

In the back of my mind I couldn't help but wonder if the current burst of resolve the man was demonstrating would fade under the pressure of everyday life. And if he did slip back into his old ways and Scooter was living all the way in Los Angeles, who would be there to rescue him from a lifestyle no kid should be forced to endure?

I knew the situation was out of my hands, so I tried not to worry about what was going to happen, though at times it was more than just a little bit hard.

On the investigation front, things were at a standstill. Willa had been questioned by the state police and released. Salinger still didn't have the whole story, but apparently, there had been a similar murder in a nearby town and Willa had just happened to be there at the time, visiting her sister. I'm sure the only reason she was even on the radar of the state police was because she'd been questioned in Candy's death, and if they'd really had anything on her they wouldn't have let her go, so I was assuming she was innocent. Deep down I didn't think Willa was a killer, especially not a serial killer, though the fact of her having been in both towns and being the last person to have been in Candy Kane's Bakeshop before Levi and I found Candy's body seemed a bit too coincidental.

I still hadn't figured out who the man Jeremy had seen with Candy was or who might have been in the kitchen. Jeremy had given a description of the man to a sketch artist in the sheriff's office, but so far Salinger hadn't found a match. Salinger had also checked Candy's employee files only to determine that she didn't have any. At least not any she'd hired legally. There was always the chance that she was paying someone under the table to help out in the kitchen.

I'd gone back to the boutique on Monday to buy the sweater and scarf for Ellie that I had on hold but was unable to chat with Betty, who had been working at the store the night Candy died. Like so many others in town, she was home sick with the flu. I'd been told she didn't want to miss any workdays so she'd traded shifts with another employee and would be working the Friday through Sunday shift this week, which turned out to be Friday through Saturday because Christmas fell on Sunday. I planned to go back to the store to have a chat with her after we'd delivered the toys the following day.

While the situation with Scooter and the identity of Candy's killer were both very much on my mind, I had twenty volunteers coming to the house to wrap the several hundred toys Alex and her group had collected. Some were being delivered to a charity in Bryton Lake, while others were going to local families to be hand delivered by a volunteer group of which I was a part.

"Do you think we have enough snacks?" Ellie asked me.

I looked at the banquet table that was overflowing with sweets and hot and cold appetizers and assured her we had more than enough to feed an army if necessary.

"It felt good to be back in the kitchen, doing what I love and feeling energetic enough to enjoy it," Ellie commented.

"I'm glad you're feeling better. I, on the other hand, am exhausted."

"You've had a long, emotional week."

"Yeah, I really have. But I'm excited about this wrapping party and ready to do my part. Do you think we have enough pairs of scissors? Maybe I should have Zak run out and get a few more."

"We have plenty. Everyone can share. I love the wrapping paper Phyllis picked out. It brings home the warmth of the season. I can just picture gifts wrapped in that paper nestled under trees all over Ashton Falls."

"It really is nice paper." I looked around the room. It looked like everything was ready. All I needed to do was change out of my sweats and put on something festive and cheery. Ellie and Alex seemed to have things handled downstairs, so I hurried up the stairs to change before everyone arrived. When I went into the bedroom Zak was putting on his heavy boots.

"Are you going out?"

"I'm heading to the Christmas store. When I was walking the dogs earlier I noticed there's a bare spot just off the back deck. I thought I'd get a few more of those mechanical reindeer we have out front."

"You know you don't need to cover every inch of ground with decorations."

"I know, but I figured if I appeared to be busy I wouldn't get rooked into wrapping gifts when your army of volunteers arrives."

I laughed. "I get it. It's going to be overwhelming and a couple more reindeer will really pull things together. Are you taking Scooter with you?"

"His dad is picking him up for the day. He should be here any minute."

"Have you had any indication from him as to what he's thinking at this point?"

Zak looked up and gave me a look of sympathy. "Not really, but if I had to guess I'd say he's leaning toward taking him to L.A."

I tried to smile, but my intention couldn't quite make it to my face. I kissed Zak good-bye and then headed to the shower.

By the time I arrived downstairs the volunteers had begun to arrive. Alex seemed like she had everything under control, so I let her take the lead while I kept busy serving snacks and refilling beverages. It was nice to have a chance to visit with the friends and family who had shown up to help. The house was warm and cozy, with just the right holiday feel.

"I have to hand it to Alex. She's done a wonderful job organizing everything," my mom commented when I brought her a fresh cup of hot cider.

"She took her time and planned everything out. That girl has a bright future ahead of her, whatever she winds up doing."

"Is she still talking about being a veterinarian?"

"She is, but Zak thinks she should focus on mathematics or one of the physical sciences. If I know Alex, she'll follow her heart, but she's only twelve. A lot can change by the time she goes to college."

"Your dad thinks Harper should be a doctor because she's constantly asking to listen to everyone's heart with the toy stethoscope we bought her," Mom said, referring to my baby sister.

"She's only two. I'm sure her interests will change many times before she's an adult."

"I'm sure they will. When I mention that to your dad, though, he tells me that he knew you would work with animals from the time you were a toddler."

"I guess I always knew in my heart that was what I was meant to do. I had so many stuffed animals when I was younger that you couldn't even find my bed."

"Harper has her eye on a fuzzy bunny at the store. I might get it for her as an extra gift."

"Let me get it for her. I still haven't finished my shopping."

"It's the purple one with the pink ears."

"A purple bunny?"

"That's the one she wants."

I guess the heart wants what the heart wants. "What time should we come over on Saturday?"

"I'm serving dinner around five, but come as early as you like. I'm really excited about Christmas this year. Harper is finally at an age when she sort of gets it. She's so excited about Santa, even if she did cry when we took her to see the one at Hometown Christmas."

"Yeah, well, the Santa at Hometown Christmas was an idiot."

"It looks like Hazel is flagging you down and I'd better get back to wrapping. If you decide not to get the purple bunny let me know."

"I'll get it," I promised.

Mom headed back to her wrapping station and I crossed the room to speak to Hazel, who had a bow stuck in her hair.

"It looked like you were waving to me."

"I was. I need some more tape and Alex isn't sure where you put it."

I seemed to remember seeing a bag with tape and other supplies in the den, so I offered to go fetch it. When I got there I found Ellie on the phone.

I waited for her to hang up before I came all the way into the room.

"Sorry. That was my doctor. He wants me to come in next week for some tests."

"Is everything okay?"

"Yeah. I think the tests are just a precaution."

I hoped Ellie was right about the tests being routine, but I thought she looked a little worried.

"If something was wrong you'd tell me?"

"Of course. You're my best friend. I tell you everything."

Ellie hugged me and left the room. Maybe I was just being overemotional, but the little voice in my head was telling me everything might not be as okay as Ellie wanted me to believe.

"I think we're going to need a bigger bus," Phyllis said as the two of us looked at the huge pile of gifts we'd wrapped. Phyllis and I planned to each take a small group of volunteers to deliver them the following day.

"I was looking at the list Alex has and I think we might need a couple of trucks and extra carrying power. You and I did it last year, but the girls outdid themselves with the toy drive this year. I think I'm going to ask Zak to bring his truck to join my group."

"Ethan has a truck and will probably be willing to help. I'll ask him. I'm sure we can get everything delivered in a few hours if we have enough people."

After Phyllis agreed to my plan I headed outside to find my holly, jolly husband.

"Hey, Christmas man." I wrapped my arms around Zak from behind while he attached a new reindeer to a circuit breaker.

"Did you get all your wrapping done?"

"We did. The girls did an awesome job this year; so awesome, in fact, that we need extra help delivering everything tomorrow. You in?"

Zak turned around and kissed me on my cold nose. "For you, anything. Do you think I should have gone ahead and bought four deer? Three seems lopsided."

"If you put the odd deer in the front it will look perfect. Although…"

"Although…?"

"Five might be better."

Zak grinned. He looked like a kid who had just been ordered to go crazy at the candy store. "Five would be better. I'll go now. Do you want to come?"

"There are still a few people here. They should be gone by the time you get back. I'll help you finish installing everything." I looked at the sea of colored lights and moving objects. "Do you think we're going to blow more than a fuse?"

Zak took my hand and led me over to a shed. Inside were two large generators. It seemed my genius of a husband really had thought of everything.

As soon as everyone was gone, I set about clearing up the room. Alex had wanted to go home with Phyllis again, which I could understand, considering she and Phyllis's three girls were the hearts and the brains behind the toy drive. I wasn't sure if Scooter would be home for dinner. I thought I'd wait to make a decision about what to cook until Zak got back from the Christmas store. The house seemed so quiet now that everyone had left. I decided to take the three dogs out for a quick run.

There were flurries in the air, but not enough to hinder my progress. I'd heard it was supposed to storm overnight, leaving up to four new inches of snow. That might mean a late start for our deliveries in the morning, but if there was one thing I knew I absolutely didn't control it was the weather, so I put it out of my mind.

I still hadn't decided what to get Zak for Christmas and it was only a few days away. I'd considered a few things, but nothing seemed quite right. I guess every year couldn't be the one you happened across the item you knew the man you loved would remember for the rest of his life. The problem was that Zak was such a sweet, thoughtful gift giver himself that I really wanted to get him something memorable.

Zak's dog, Bella, and Scooter's dog, Digger, were wrestling over a stick, but my sweet little Charlie preferred to trot along at my side. I wondered if Scooter's dad would let Scooter take Digger with him if he decided to take him to L.A. It would kill both Scooter and Digger to be parted from each other for any significant amount of time. I bent down and picked up a clump of snow. I formed it into a snowball and threw it into the lake as hard as I could. Just the thought of Scooter leaving us filled me with pain and frustration I didn't have an outlet to unleash.

I found a log that was partially sheltered by a large evergreen tree and decided to take a break. I sat down facing the lake and pulled Charlie into my lap. I buried my frozen face into his warm fur and let go of the tears I'd been holding at bay. I was trying to remain strong for Scooter, Alex, and Zak, but when it came right down to it, I wasn't feeling strong at all. Charlie whimpered and licked my face. I knew he could tell I was upset.

"It's okay. I'm okay." I forced a smile. "See. Happy as can be."

Charlie barked. I was pretty sure he was calling me out as a liar.

"The snow is getting harder. Should we head back?"

Charlie let out a whine.

"Yeah. It probably is a good idea. I bet Zak is home by now. He's probably wondering where we've gone off to."

I called Bella and Digger and headed back toward the house. One thing was for certain: No one would be lost in the woods as long as Zak had his light display up. It was snowing pretty hard by now and I was a good quarter mile from home, but still the sky shone brightly like a beacon in the coming darkness.

I'd almost reached the house when my phone rang.

"Salinger."

"Donovan."

"You have news?"

"You alone?"

I looked around. I certainly was if you didn't count the dogs. "Yeah, I can talk. What's up?"

"A good citizen who wishes to remain anonymous found a bank bag full of cash in a snowbank in the alley behind Candy Kane's Bakeshop."

"A bank bag? That makes no sense. The murder was a week ago. Why would the bag just be found now?"

"It was snowing the day Ms. Kane died and it snowed hard that night too, so my theory is that the bag was buried in the snowbank and wasn't visible until the county came through to widen the roads in anticipation of the snow we're expecting to get tonight."

"I guess it could have happened that way. But if Candy *was* killed in the course of a robbery, why did the thief dump the bag in the first place?"

"Maybe there was someone in the alley and he or she didn't want to be seen with the loot."

"Okay, then why not go back for it before now? As I said, it's been a week."

"Good question. Which brings me to theory number two. Someone did steal the cash but didn't kill Candy Kane. When they heard about it they didn't want to be linked to the murder scene, so they turned in the cash pretending to be good citizens who found the bank bag."

I waved to Digger, who was beginning to wander away. "That sort of makes sense, but unless the cash was traceable somehow, I'm not sure how keeping the cash would have led us back to the person who took it."

"Yeah, the theory is a stretch."

"Can you get prints off the money or the bag?"

"We're on it. Any news on your end?"

"No. I've been too busy with Christmas, family, and a toy drive to put much effort into it," I admitted.

"That's understandable given the situation with Scooter."

"You heard?"

"I did. Anything I can do?"

"No. Scooter's dad is well within his legal rights to take Scooter with him if he wants to."

"I have a long history on file of drunk and disorderly conduct."

"Yeah. But that was before. He seems better. It would be pretty low to use that now. Besides, Zak and I have talked it over and mostly agree that being reunited with his dad might actually be a good thing for Scooter in the long run."

"Yeah, I think you're right. Listen, I know you're busy with family obligations, but if you hear anything keep me in the loop."

"Of course," I promised. "Oh, did you ever backtrack to find out where Candy had been before moving to Ashton Falls?"

"I did. After Candy Davenport was accused of poisoning her husband she changed her name to Candy Kane and opened a small candy store in Florida. Two years ago she moved to Bryton Lake and got a job at a large bakery in the mall; three months ago she moved to Ashton Falls and opened Candy Kane's Bakeshop. She was still considered the prime suspect in the death of her husband, but the case went cold when they couldn't find enough evidence to arrest her. Here's the really interesting thing: The town where Candy lived with her husband has a new sheriff who happens to be married to Donny Davenport's niece. He began digging into the case right around the time Candy left Bryton Lake behind and moved here."

"So Candy killed her husband and left town. Eventually the case grew cold until the new sheriff, who happened to be married to the victim's niece, began digging around. I guess we can assume this new sheriff tracked Candy to Bryton Lake, which made her quit her job and move to Ashton Falls."

"That's the way it looks to me."

"It still doesn't tell us who killed her. What about the other death? The one the state police are looking in to?"

"Willa's sister provided an alibi for her for the time of the murder that occurred upstate."

"Upstate? As in the town where Candy grew up?"

"No. The murder the state police are investigating took place in a small town about thirty miles east of the town where Candy grew up. The person I spoke to from the state police didn't have any reason to think the two cases were related until he did some digging and found out about not only Candy's history but the fact that Willa had been present in both locations at the times of death."

"So there are actually three deaths that seem like they could be connected in some way? Do you think they are?"

"I suppose it may turn out all these random events are linked in some way, but it's just as likely Candy's death really was simply the result of a robbery."

Unfortunately, it sounded like Salinger was no closer to solving the case than he'd been when we started.

Chapter 9

Later that evening I curled up on the sofa in front of the fire with Charlie and the household cats. Zak and Scooter were in the den playing video games, so I took a few minutes to write down some notes, trying to find a degree of focus on the murder case. I looked at the list I'd been keeping and tried to decide who I could cross off and who needed to stay.

My first thought had been that Candy had died during the execution of a robbery. The fact that Candy's bank bag had been found in the snow behind her shop seemed to give a bit of legitimacy to that theory, despite a number of remaining unanswered questions. We had no idea who had taken the cash, who had turned it in, whether it had been found where the anonymous source said it was, and whether the cash was related to Candy's death. Still, *person who robbed store* was now my number-one suspect.

The second and third suspects on my list were Veronica from Veronica's Bakery and her cousin Kevin. Both seemed to have motive, but they also seemed to have alibis, so I crossed them off for the moment.

Next on my list was the neighbor with the yapping dog. Salinger had indicated that he'd spoken to her, and while she'd been home alone, she'd spoken to a friend on her landline, which provided an alibi of sorts. I supposed if she'd had a strong motive I'd have looked into this further, but if she'd wanted to kill Candy why go to her bakery to do it? She did, after all, live right next door.

Clarissa Vanderbilt of Granny's Quilts had been out of town at the time of the murder, and while it was possible one or more of the women from the quilting circle that had been displaced when the shop closed could have killed Candy, it seemed unlikely; I crossed Clarissa off the suspect list as well.

Levi had also spoken to Nick Benson, who'd been home alone at the time of the killing and didn't have an alibi. Technically, I suppose I should have him on the list, but I couldn't quite force myself to add him to it, so I jotted his name down as a side note.

I also wanted to skip the addition of Willa Walton, a woman I knew and admired, but the fact that she'd been seen leaving the shop minutes before Levi and I arrived there forced me to consider her a suspect until such time as the killer was found or the theory that she might have killed Candy in a fit of rage was disproved.

Jerry from the Mexican restaurant had seemed nervous when I'd spoken to him, so I left him on the list. Could he have come by for a visit, as he'd been known to do, and then found himself in an altercation of some sort with his old friend? He hadn't seemed inclined to share much with me, so I wondered how I could find out more about both the past and more recent relationship he'd had with Candy.

And then there was the man with the red hair who'd been in the bakery chatting with Candy when Jeremy was there picking up his order just an hour or so before she died, as well as whoever was in the kitchen. Jeremy had indicated that Candy seemed nervous. Could either the man in the booth or the person in the kitchen have been responsible for her death?

Once I'd organized my list of suspects I made a list of people I still wanted to follow up with. On the top of that list was Betty from the boutique, who would have been working next door on the night Candy died. It seemed reasonable that she might have heard what was going on.

I was also curious to find out who had seen Willa leaving the bakery that night. So far not a single person I'd spoken to had admitted to have seen or heard anything, yet someone had informed Salinger that Willa had been on the premises. Could it have been someone from one of the nearby shops or someone lurking in the alley?

While it seemed totally plausible that Candy had been killed during the course of a robbery or by a disgruntled Ashton Falls native, I also needed to consider whether Candy's death could have been the result of her past. As far as I could tell, Candy had not only moved around quite a few times but she had at least one alias as well. I wasn't sure how much luck I'd have trying to track down Candy's sister, Janell, but perhaps it might be worth my while to try.

"Why the serious expression?" Zak asked as he sat down next to me.

"I'm trying to figure out who killed Candy."

Zak took the notebook out of my hands and tossed it onto a nearby table. "I don't think you'll be able to solve this particular crime tonight, so why don't we try to relax and enjoy the fire and the decorations?"

I leaned my head on Zak's shoulder as I looked at the flames that almost seemed to dance to the melody of the Christmas music. The colorful decorations combined with the fire, music, and scent of bayberry candles really did provide a cozy and romantic atmosphere. Zak was right. Thoughts of murder and motive could wait.

"Did Scooter go to bed?"

"He went up to his room. I think he's watching TV."

"How did he seem tonight?"

"Seem?"

"Did it seem like he was worried or upset?" My heart really did ache when I thought of the uncertainty the poor boy was having to live with.

"Scooter seems to be able to compartmentalize the situation better now that things have settled into something of a routine for the time being. When we were playing video games he seemed to be totally into killing off my robots and didn't appear to have anything else on his mind."

"I guess that's good. I'd hate to see him stressed out over Christmas."

Zak pulled me into his arms. "Which is exactly how I feel about you."

I snuggled closer to his warm body. "I guess I have been stressing lately, over this murder and over what's going to happen with Scooter. I guess I've even been stressing over the advice I gave Levi, wondering if it was good or bad."

"What advice?"

I tucked my feet up under my body as Zak pulled a throw over our laps. "Levi bought Ellie an engagement ring for Christmas. I told him it was too soon to give it to her. I was sure she wasn't ready, and maybe she isn't, but they seem to be getting along really well lately, so I might have been premature in offering advice on the subject."

"I know you care about both Levi and Ellie, and I know you want them both to be happy, but don't you think you should let them figure out their own relationship?"

I didn't answer, though I was beginning to think staying out of the Levi/Ellie dynamic really was the right thing to do.

"What time do we need to be ready in the morning?" Zak asked.

"Phyllis and the girls are coming by at ten. Hopefully, the deliveries won't take too long. Can you believe it will be Christmas Eve in just two days? It seems like this holiday season has flown by."

"Isn't it like that most years?"

"Yeah, I guess. I just feel like we haven't really done anything yet."

"Like what?"

"Like take a sleigh ride or go into town to look at the windows. Hometown Christmas seemed like a blur with all the sick volunteers combined with the murder investigation."

Zak tucked a lock of hair behind my ear. "Why don't we have a family night tomorrow? I'll rent us a sleigh and we can head into town and look at the windows and maybe have dinner."

I smiled. "I'd like that."

"I'll ask Scooter's dad if he can have him back here by five. I know Alex has been asking about ice skating. Maybe we can do that too."

"It sounds like exactly the type of Christmas magic we need."

Zak and I continued to snuggle in front of the fire as music played in the background. It was nice to relax and turn off my mind completely. It really had been a stressful week; taking a mental break was exactly what I needed.

"Are you up for a Christmas movie?" Zak asked.

"That sounds nice. Something light and funny. I think I've had enough drama in my life."

Zak got up and began to sort through the movies we owned while I went into the kitchen to make popcorn. I was looking in the cabinet for a bowl when the phone rang.

"Is this Zoe Donovan?" a female voice asked.

"It is."

"The Zoe Donovan who's looking into the murder of the bakery owner?"

"Yes. I'm that Zoe Donovan. Who is this?"

"A concerned citizen who prefers to remain anonymous."

I grabbed a pad and pen from a nearby drawer in case I needed to jot down something the caller was going to say. "Do you have some information that will help me?"

"I was in the alley the night the bakery owner died. I saw the lady from the county both enter and leave the bakery just before you showed up with the dark-haired man."

"Yes, we know the woman from the county was at the bakery just before we got there."

"Did you know there was someone else there as well?"

"Someone else?"

"A woman. I didn't get a good look at her. It was dark and she had on a dark cape. The sort with a hood."

"And this woman came out of the bakery?"

"I didn't see her come out, but I saw her go in."

"Before the woman from the county?"

"Yes. Maybe five minutes before."

I frowned. "So as far as you know, this woman with the cape was still inside the bakery when Willa, the woman from the county, arrived?"

"I didn't see her leave."

If there had been someone inside the bakery when Willa showed up, wouldn't Willa have seen her? Something didn't seem right. Of course I had no reason to believe this anonymous caller, although I had no reason to doubt her either.

"Are you the one who called in the anonymous tip about the woman from the county being at the bakery to the sheriff?"

The woman paused. "No. You're the only person I've called. I wasn't going to call at all, but I was telling a friend what I saw and she encouraged me to tell you."

"Is there a reason you don't want to tell me who you are?"

"It's safer that way. I really need to go."

"Wait. Can you tell me anything at all about the woman with the cape? Like maybe her height and general build?"

"She was petite. Maybe your size. The cape hid a lot, but she seemed thin. I hope you find whoever did this. I don't feel safe with a killer on the loose."

The woman hung up.

"Strange." I hung up the phone, then grabbed the bag of popcorn from the microwave. I poured it into a cute bowl with a snowman on it and added some salt. By the time I returned to the living room Zak had a movie cued up and ready to go.

"Did I hear the phone ring?"

"It was a woman with a tip about Candy's murder," I informed Zak. I spent the next few minutes filling him in on what she had shared. "She began the conversation as if she didn't know me. She wanted to know if I was Zoe Donovan, and if I was the one looking into the murder. But when I asked her about the woman with the cape she said she was petite, about my size."

"So she knows you."

"She must know me well enough to know I'm petite."

"Isn't this at least the third anonymous caller to come forward? Do you think it's the same person?"

"I don't know. I asked her if she was the one who'd informed Salinger that Willa had been seen leaving the scene of the crime and she said no, I was the first person she called. I didn't think to ask her if she was the one who turned in the money."

"I suppose there might be three different concerned citizens, but it seems if the person who called Salinger and the one who called you aren't the same, they would have been in the alley at the same time and would most likely have seen each other."

"That makes sense."

I sat down next to Zak. I offered him some of the popcorn, but he waited to start the movie. "If the woman on the phone was both accurate and truthful, the woman with the cape would have been inside the bakery when Willa got there. Wouldn't you think she would have seen her?"

"I suppose if we believe she didn't look in the pantry, which is what she claimed, the woman with the cape could have been in the pantry with Candy."

"If that's true she has to be the killer."

Chapter 10

Friday, December 23

Zak and I were teamed up with Alex and Pepper the following day. Pepper was a sixteen-year-old bundle of energy who attended Zimmerman Academy and lived with Phyllis and two other students.

"I'm having the best time. Aren't you having the best time?" Pepper rambled as she scooted into the backseat of the truck next to Alex after we'd completed our first drop-off.

"It is fun to make people smile," Alex agreed.

"I swear, the woman was waiting by the window for us to arrive. She opened the door before we even had a chance to ring the bell."

"We got there right when I told her we would."

Alex and Eve had called ahead to all the homes and arranged approximate delivery times for each family. Some of the parents wanted to be sure the kids weren't home when the packages arrived so they could claim the shiny new toys actually came from the white-bearded man up north.

"Did you see how happy that lady was when Zak came in with the bike for her son?" Pepper continued. "I don't know that I've ever seen a smile quite that big."

"The Smiths are new to Ashton Falls," Alex explained. "I think when I called to set up the delivery Mrs. Smith just assumed we'd be dropping off a few used toys rather than brand-new ones matched to each child in the family."

"It's really nice that you and Eve have gone to so much trouble. Ashton Falls really is the best place to be at Christmas."

"Did you talk to your dad to confirm whether you're going home or staying?" Alex asked.

"I'm staying," Pepper said. "I knew before I even called my dad that he would think it best if I didn't interfere with his new family. I wouldn't even have bothered to verify that he wouldn't be sending for me, but I'm hoping my poor-me routine made him feel guilty enough to come through with the new convertible I've had my eye on."

Poor Pepper. She acted like it was no big deal that her father didn't want her to spend Christmas with him and his new family, but I knew it bothered her a lot more than she let on.

"You want to get a convertible in Ashton Falls?" Alex asked.

Pepper looked out the window at the snow that had just begun to fall. "I guess a convertible isn't all that practical in the winter, but it sure would be fun in the summer."

"Are we going over to Seventh Street or Aspen Court next?" Zak asked Alex as he navigated through town.

"Let's head over to Aspen. There are three deliveries within a few blocks. We can loop back around to Seventh."

Zak made the turn while Alex and Pepper continued to chat loud enough to be heard over the Christmas carols playing on the radio. It really was a perfect day to make the Santa run. It was snowing enough to add atmosphere but not so hard as to be a deterrent to driving the often-narrow streets.

By the time we'd delivered the last gift it was well into midafternoon. Phyllis and Ethan's team still had a few deliveries left to make, so we decided to take both girls back to our place, where they could hang out until Phyllis came by to pick up Pepper. I was excited about our family night that evening, but first I wanted to head over to the boutique to have a chat with Betty if she had indeed come in that day.

"Betty?" I asked the woman behind the counter when I walked into the otherwise empty store.

"That's me. Can I help you?"

"My name is Zoe. I was in earlier in the week asking store owners about the night Candy Kane was killed and was told you were working that night."

"Yes, I was."

"You were just on the other side of the wall from where Candy was murdered. I wondered if you heard anything."

"No, not a sound. These are pretty thick walls. Even when the bakery was open we didn't get a lot of noise in here."

"Did you notice anyone around? Maybe someone lurking in the alley?"

"I didn't see a thing."

I looked at the woman, who was both petite and thin. There was a dark cape with a hood hanging on the coatrack. "Someone called me last night to inform me that a woman of about your height wearing a cape that was described as looking like the one hanging on that coatrack was seen entering the bakery through the back door on the night Candy died."

The woman frowned. She paused for just a minute before she answered. "If I tell you something, you have to promise to keep it to yourself."

"I guess I can do that as long as it doesn't hinder tracking down the killer."

"We aren't supposed to leave the store if we're here alone and we aren't supposed to smoke, so occasionally, if things are slow, I'll lock the front door and sneak out back for a quick smoke."

I waited to see if the woman would add anything that might be relevant.

"On the night the woman next door was murdered I popped out into the alley for a quick break and when I came back through the bakery I had a feeling someone was there. I guess that must have been the person who saw me."

"You went back through the bakery?"

She looked around, as if making sure we were still alone. "The back door of the boutique has an alarm. I know the code to turn it off, but there's a log that lets the owners know if and when the alarm has been deactivated. We really aren't supposed to open the back door except for scheduled deliveries and emergencies. You might not know it by looking, but some of these clothes are very pricey. I think the owner is afraid her merchandise might disappear through the back door if she doesn't keep a close eye on it."

The sweater I'd bought for Ellie had put me back a pretty penny, so I had no doubt many of the dresses and especially the shoes ran several thousand dollars apiece. No wonder the store was always empty. Who in Ashton Falls could afford to dress like that?

"Anyway, if the bakery is open the woman who works there let me go in and out through her alley door," Betty continued.

"There's a door between the two shops?"

"Yes. It's behind that storage area over there. Our side door opens into a small hallway between her kitchen and dining area. On the night Candy died I noticed her light was on, so I used the door to grab a smoke."

"Did you see Candy when you went out into the alley?"

"No. I guess I should have realized it was odd that the lights were on and Candy wasn't in the kitchen, but she was known to grab a smoke now and then herself, so I just figured she'd gone out for a moment."

"Was the door leading from her kitchen to the alley unlocked?"

"Yes. I had my cigarette and then came back through the bakery to the boutique. As I said, I didn't see anyone, but it felt as if someone was there. You know how you get a chill on the back of your neck when someone's watching you?"

"And you were wearing that black cape?"

"I was. I hope whoever saw me doesn't tell my boss I was in the alley. I'll get fired for sure."

"I don't think they knew who you were." I paused to gather my thoughts. "How long were you in the alley?"

"Five minutes. Ten at the most."

So Betty must have left the bakery before my anonymous caller arrived. She must have entered the picture shortly after, though, because she was there in time to see Betty return to the boutique through the bakery. Willa appeared not long after that, and shortly after Willa left, Levi and I arrived. It seemed like a pretty tight timeline, considering Candy's death couldn't have been very long before Betty went out for her break.

"Thanks for your time. If you think of anything else, please call me."

"You should talk to Jerry."

"Jerry who washes dishes at the Mexican restaurant?"

"Yes. He hung out in the bakery pretty often. At first I thought he was hooking up with Candy, who's way older than him, but then I figured something else must have been going on."

"Something else?"

"Drugs. Pies and cookies weren't the only things Candy was selling."

"Are you sure?"

"Well, no," Betty admitted. "But there was something seedy going on. I'm sure of it."

I called Salinger and filled him in on the drug angle. The sale of drugs in the bakery could be an important clue if it was true. He kind of doubted Candy had been selling drugs but said he'd look into it.

"Did you ever manage to get any prints from the money in the bank bag?" I asked.

"Too many. It's money; it's been around. I did manage to get a couple of prints off the bag. Here's the strange thing, though: While I haven't been able to match either print, neither print belonged to Candy."

"Huh? That makes no sense."

"Here's where we are: An anonymous person found a bank bag full of cash in the alley behind the bakeshop, so we assumed it had belonged to Candy. What if it didn't? There's nothing either on the bag or inside it to identify the owner."

"Or," I postulated, "what if the cash is some kind of a decoy?"

"A decoy?"

"The real killer wants us to think Candy was killed during a robbery so they planted the cash to throw us off."

"I guess it could have happened that way. It did seem odd that the person who turned the cash in wanted to remain anonymous."

"This investigation seems to be going nowhere, but at least we can cross Willa off the suspect list."

"Cross Willa off? Why?"

"Betty, the woman who works in the boutique next door to the bakery, used the door that connects the two shops to leave the building on the night Candy was killed. She was seen returning to the boutique just a few minutes before Willa arrived by another anonymous caller. Betty told me that she didn't see Candy in the kitchen when she slipped through and figured she had slipped out for her own cigarette break. Given the tight timeline and the fact that my anonymous source saw Betty return to the bakery and Willa arrive and leave, it seems Candy must have been already dead before Willa arrived."

"So are we thinking this Betty might have killed her?"

"She would have had opportunity because she was able to go back and forth between the boutique and the bakery, but I didn't pick up on any sort of motive. We can add her to the suspect list and look into her story further, though. By the way, did you have any luck tracking down Candy's sister Janell?"

"Not yet. Maybe you can ask your computer-genius husband to work on that."

"My computer-genius husband and I are taking the kids out for family night tonight. I'll mention it to him tomorrow, if he has time."

"Tracking down the sister might help us understand exactly what Candy was up to before she moved to Ashton Falls. If he is up to it, tell him to call me and I'll fill him in on what I've managed to find out. Oh, I found out who the redheaded man Jeremy saw talking to Candy on the night she died was."

"Really? Who?"

"A private detective who works out of Edgewood. He was hired by Donny Davenport's niece to do some of the legwork on the poisoning case."

"I guess that explains why she seemed nervous."

"Yeah, it does. Have fun tonight."

"I will."

"And Donovan…Leave the interview with this Jerry fellow to me. If he was dealing drugs with Candy, he might be dangerous. I don't want you putting yourself into any situations where you might get hurt."

"You mean as opposed to pretty much every other murder I've investigated?"

"Exactly."

Chapter 11

I can't begin to tell you how wonderful it felt to have the family together for a night on the town. Alex and I had a blast looking at all the windows along Main while Zak and Scooter tagged along after us, eating junk food and talking about the new video game Zak's ward, Pi, was developing. Pi was in college this year and I'd hoped he'd come home for the holiday, but he had a new girlfriend who seemed to take precedence over spending his break in Ashton Falls. I was upset about it at first, but Zak had pointed out that Pi was almost eighteen, and as a young adult out on his own for the first time, he was naturally inclined to want to exert his independence to a certain degree.

"My favorite window so far is the one with the North Pole zoo," Alex commented. "I really loved the polar bears."

"That was a cute window. The one with the ski resort was pretty cute too."

"We have so many decorations; why don't we have a village?" Alex wondered.

A village we could add to each year would be fun. "We could put it in the bay window off the kitchen."

"It would be fun to pick out special pieces."

I stopped walking and turned to look at Zak. "What do you think? Are you up for another trip to the Christmas store?"

"I don't want to go to the Christmas store. When can we go to the sledding hill?" Scooter whined.

"How about I take Scooter sledding and you girls can go to the Christmas store? Just have the store hold whatever you buy and I'll bring the truck around to pick it up. After that we'll have dinner."

I looked at Alex. "It's okay with me."

"Sure, that sounds like fun, but let's not forget we were going to go ice skating after dinner."

We parted ways and Alex and I headed toward the only store in town that specialized in seasonal items. The entire downtown section of Ashton Falls was crowded with holiday shoppers out looking for last-minute items to complete their holiday shopping.

"I need to stop off at the store to pick up a gift for Harper. We'll pass right by there, so let's stop first so I don't forget."

"What are you getting her?"

"A purple bunny."

Alex turned and grinned at me.

"That's what my mom insisted she wants."

"Purple bunnies are cool. My parents never let me have a bunch of stuffed animals when I was young. It was too hard to travel with them."

"Well, you've certainly made up for that now."

"As long as we're stopping at Donovan's, I want to look for something for Scooter." Alex slipped her hand into mine. "I want to find something special. Something he can remember me by if his dad takes him away."

I squeezed Alex's hand. I could hear the catch in her voice. I guess I hadn't given all that much thought to how this was affecting her.

"We'll look until we find the perfect thing," I promised.

"At first I thought about getting him one of those superfast sleds he's always talking about, but I guess it doesn't snow in L.A."

"No, I guess it doesn't."

"Do you think Scooter will be able to come visit us if he has to move?"

"I'm sure he will."

"But it won't be the same."

I felt a catch in my own throat. "No. It won't."

I let go of Alex's hand as we entered the festive but crowded interior of the store. The place was packed. Maybe this hadn't been such a good idea. By the time we waited in line we'd never have time to go to the Christmas store. Of course tomorrow was Christmas Eve. If Alex and I were going to finish our shopping it was going to have to be now. I'd just text Zak to tell him to take his time sledding.

Luckily, there was one purple bunny left on the pile, which I grabbed and placed in my cart before anyone else had a chance to get it. Maybe I'd pick up a stuffed toy for Ellie and Levi's baby too, as long as I was at it. Alex helped me sort through the pile of plush toys. We settled on a monkey that felt so cuddly I almost wanted it for myself.

"Do you think Scooter would like a camera?" Alex asked. "He could take photos of his new house and his new life and send them to us."

"I think Scooter might like a camera very much."

"You know Tucker is going to be lost without him."

"Yeah. I guess he will."

"And his soccer team is never going to win the playoffs next year if they lose their best forward."

"I guess that's true too."

Alex turned her back to me, I imagined in an attempt to hide the tears I'd seen her frantically wipe away.

I wished I had the words to comfort her, but I really didn't. While it was true Scooter's dad hadn't definitely decided to take him, I had to agree with Zak that it seemed pretty likely.

"So how about we pay for this stuff and head to the Christmas store?"

"Okay."

I put my arm around Alex as we headed toward the very long line. It was hot and noisy in the store and the bright lights were giving me a headache.

"I'm going to grab a small bottle of aspirin. Save our place."

"You aren't feeling well?"

"Just a headache."

"I hope you aren't getting that flu that's been going around."

I put my hand on my stomach. I did feel a little queasy, but I'd been really stressed and really busy. I was sure I was fine. "I'll just be a minute." I ran to the pharmacy department and found the aisle with the pain relievers. I tossed in a small bottle of antacid as well. I was about to return to Alex when something else caught my eye and made me pause. Could it be?

We all pigged out on Italian food, then headed toward the ice skating rink. My heart beat a little bit faster as both kids took off running, Zak and I following behind. It was times like this that I felt like we were an old married couple, not a married couple who'd yet to have a child of our own, but I knew if we didn't have Scooter with us next year my heart would have a hole in it that no amount of Christmas magic could fill.

"Are we skating or are we going to sit in the stands and neck?" Zak asked.

"As much as I applaud the concept of necking, I'm not sure the skating rink is the most appropriate place to do that. When we get home, however, I'll be happy to take you up on your offer. In fact..." I wasn't able to finish the sentence because my phone beeped, letting me know I had a text.

I almost ignored it but decided at the last minute to check to make sure it wasn't an emergency. It was.

"What happened?" I asked Levi after dialing his number.

"I don't know. Ellie and I were sitting on the sofa watching a movie and she turned completely pale and passed out. She's in with the doctor now."

"Are you at the hospital?"

"Yeah. In emergency."

"I'll be right there."

I didn't know if the situation was serious at this point, so I decided there was no reason to disrupt the kids' fun, especially if this did end up being their last Christmas together, so Zak continued on to the skating rink while I ran as fast as I could back to the truck, then made the short trip to the hospital in record time. When I arrived in the waiting room Levi was pacing like a caged animal.

"Have you heard anything?"

"No. Not yet."

"Ellie mentioned that her doctor wanted her to have some additional tests."

Levi's lips tightened. "She didn't say anything about tests to me."

"She probably didn't want to worry you, especially if there wasn't anything to worry about. I happened to overhear her on the phone making the appointment." I placed my hand on Levi's. "Let's sit down."

"You can sit; I'm too wound up. What if something's wrong with the baby? What if Ellie's in danger?"

"I'm sure Ellie and the baby are fine." Even as I said the words, I didn't believe them myself.

Levi ran his hand through his hair. "I don't know what I'm going to do if I lose them."

"You won't lose them. Come on. Let's sit down. Making yourself crazy isn't going to help Ellie."

Levi looked like he wanted to argue with me, but he didn't. I sat down next to him and clung to his hand like a lifeline.

"How was Ellie feeling before she passed out?" I asked.

"Tired. She said she was a little light-headed. She's been so busy with Christmas and everything. But she's seemed to have a lot of energy lately. I warned her to take it easy, but she said she felt fine."

I watched the minutes on the clock on the wall tick by as we waited. Small talk seemed out of place and I don't think either of us wanted to voice the terror we felt. Christmas music played in the background, which, given the circumstances, somehow seemed wrong too.

"What's taking so long?" Levi asked.

"I don't know. Do you want me to talk to a nurse? Maybe we can find out exactly what's going on."

"I asked before you got here, but no one was talking." Levi turned and looked at me. "If we were married I could be with her."

"We don't know that for sure."

"Maybe. But I'm not taking another chance on something like this happening again. One way or another, I'm marrying that girl before the new year arrives."

I hoped Levi would calm down and not try to go all caveman on Ellie. That wasn't going to go over well at all.

Finally, after what seemed like a lifetime, a doctor came into the room. "Are you the baby's father?" He asked Levi.

"I am."

"Your baby is going to be fine. Ellie's blood pressure is a little high and some of her levels are off, but it's nothing serious. We're going to keep her overnight so we can monitor her while we get everything stabilized."

"Can I see her?" Levi asked.

"I don't see why not. But we're trying to lower her blood pressure, so before I allow you to go in you'll need to take a deep breath and get your emotions under control."

Levi took a deep breath as instructed.

"He'll be fine," I assured the doctor. "He won't do or say anything to cause Ellie any stress." I looked Levi directly in the eye.

"No," Levi promised. "I won't do or say anything to add to her stress level."

I hugged Levi and while I did, I whispered in his ear not to bring up the marriage thing at this particular time. He nodded, and I made him promise to let me know if anything changed. He agreed and followed the doctor through the double doors while I said a quick prayer of thanks before turning to the exit to rejoin my family.

"Are the kids asleep?" Zak asked when I returned to the living room after going upstairs to check on them.

"They are, and it's still early. I think we managed to tire them both out."

"You look pretty tired yourself."

"I'm just worried about Ellie. The doctor said she'd be fine, but we both know what a difficult time she'd had with all things pregnancy related."

"I'm sure the doctor wouldn't be sending her home in the morning if she wasn't fine." Zak pulled me onto his lap and cuddled me close to his chest. I watched the flames dancing in the fire as I listened to Zak's heart beat against my ear. Listening to Zak's heartbeat always made me feel safe and secure.

"So what's the plan for tomorrow?" Zak asked.

"I have to go into town. Just for a couple of hours. I still have two or three gifts to buy. I thought maybe we could go out to grab some lunch as a family before we head over to my parents. Mom's planning dinner at five, but she said to come whenever." I paused and frowned. "Will we have Scooter tomorrow? Have you spoken to his father about it?"

"Yes, but he didn't commit. He did say he wanted to stop by to speak to me in the morning. I guess we'll find out what's on his mind then."

"Stop by?" That didn't sound good. If he was fine with Scooter spending Christmas with us he could have just said so over the phone. *Stopping by* sounded like a bad-news sort of event.

Zak caressed my hair. "Don't make yourself crazy worrying about what it means. It might be nothing at all."

"I can't help it. *Stopping by* doesn't sound like a good thing."

"Maybe he just wants to ask about a gift for Scooter."

"He couldn't ask you that over the phone?"

Zak tightened his arms around me. "I hate to see you so upset. I wish I could do or say something to put your mind at ease, but I don't know how this is all going to work out."

He kissed a teardrop from my face. "Remember that first summer when I agreed to babysit Scooter in exchange for his dad's promise to drop the case against the dog that had bitten him while protecting the little girl who owned him?"

I smiled. When Zak first became involved with Scooter he was a nine-year-old tornado who tended to blow through town, destroying everything in his path. Saying Scooter was undisciplined didn't do justice to how huge a disaster the boy really had been. "I thought you were crazy. I thought Scooter was going to destroy this house and drive you completely over the edge in the process."

"I'll admit he and I had a rocky beginning." Zak laughed. "And yes, he did almost destroy the house. But we worked it out."

"Yeah." I smiled. "You really did. Scooter's dad has to see what a huge influence you've been on his son."

"He does. He's mentioned as much."

Zak continued to stroke my head as we listened to the Christmas music. Then the colors of the lights on the tree all blended together as my eyes teared up.

"I'm really scared," I whispered.

Zak tightened his arms around me. "Yeah, me too."

Chapter 12

Saturday, December 24

I decided to head into town early, before the kids got up. I wanted to spend as much time as I had left with my *whole* family. Most of the stores opened early that morning and then planned to close early so their employees could spend Christmas Eve with their families. My first stop was to Donovan's, where I picked up a few things, including Zak's gift. At least I hoped it would be Zak's gift. I wasn't a hundred percent sure it would work out, but I had my suspicions. I also picked up a few additional trinkets for Alex and Scooter, as well as some baby toys for Levi and Ellie.

I hoped Ellie would be released from the hospital this morning so I could stop by to visit with my friends before the business of the day ahead completely took over.

Once I completed my shopping I headed over to the boutique where I'd bought Ellie's scarf and sweater. I'd seen a sweater I thought Alex would like when I'd been there the last time but was unsure about spending so much money on something she would just outgrow. Still, the more I thought about it, the more I wanted her to have it, so I made up my mind to throw logic to the wind and buy it for her anyway.

"Good morning, Betty," I said when I entered the shop.

"Zoe, right? Did you have more questions?"

"No, I'm actually here about a sweater." I walked across the store to the rack in the very back, near the storeroom, where I'd seen the sweater on my previous visit. I smiled when I saw it was still there. I took it off the rack and held it up. "This sweater."

"You're in luck. That's the last one in that size."

"Fantastic. Can you wrap it? I want the package to be something special."

"Absolutely. I have paper in the back. Just give me a minute."

I smiled at the woman as she walked through the door and into the storeroom. When I'd woken up that morning I'd vowed to myself that I was going to have a good day no matter what else happened. It was, after all, Christmas Eve. A day for joy and celebration.

I looked around the boutique while I waited for Betty to return. It was a cute little shop, even if it was over-the-top expensive. I picked up a silk blouse that was on the sale rack but didn't have a tag on it. I took it with me as I headed to the storeroom.

"I found this blouse on the sale rack. I was wondering…" I stopped talking.

Betty followed my gaze, which was locked on a bloody rolling pin sticking out from under a pile of discarded boxes stashed in the corner.

"You," I said. "You killed Candy."

Betty turned and looked at me. It only took a second for me to realize she had a small gun in her hand.

"Why?" I asked.

"She killed Donny. She told everyone she didn't, but she did."

I remembered Donny was the name of the husband who had died.

"Was Donny a friend of yours?"

"More than a friend."

I paused as I allowed my brain to catch up with the ideas swirling around me. Betty had killed Candy. She must have gotten into the bakery through the connecting door, hit her over the head with the rolling pin that probably had been on the counter to roll out the dough for the sugar cookies, paused outside for a smoke, and then returned to work, which was when my witness had seen her enter the building.

"You were lovers?" I finally asked.

"More than lovers. Donny loved me. He was going to leave his bitch of a wife for me. When I found out he'd been poisoned I knew she did it. Everyone did. But the sheriff couldn't prove it, and then she disappeared."

"And when you found out she was in Ashton Falls you applied for a job at the boutique next door. Did Candy recognize you?"

"No. She never knew about me."

My ears began to ring as the room started to spin. I knew I was going to pass out, but I had no idea what I could do to stop it. I grabbed for the wall behind me as everything went dark. The next thing I knew I woke up in the pantry of Candy's Bakeshop. My hands and feet were tied, but at least I wasn't dead.

I managed to scoot into a sitting position. I was kind of surprised to find I was still alive. I was sure Betty planned to shoot me, but for some reason she'd stashed me in the bakery instead.

I looked around the room, trying to decide what to do. My hands and feet were tied securely and there was duct tape over my mouth. There was loud music coming from the T-shirt shop next door. I doubted the people inside would hear me, but maybe if I could make my way through the kitchen and over to the connecting wall I could pound on the wall loud enough to get someone's attention.

On the other hand, maybe Betty was waiting in the kitchen for me to wake up and I was better off pretending I hadn't regained consciousness while I tried to work the ropes free.

I decided to simply sit still and breathe deeply through my nose until the dizziness left me completely. I wasn't sure how long I'd been in the pantry, but I didn't think it could be too long.

"I've searched high and low, but I can't find the cash. I think we should just assume it was never here and Candy lied. I really think we should forget about it and leave town," a voice that sounded like Betty's insisted. I could hear footsteps and realized someone had come into the bakery through the connecting door.

"Did you look behind the air vents?" a male voice asked.

"I've looked everywhere. And I mean everywhere. Maybe she never had the money," Betty repeated.

The man cleared his throat. "This is your fault, you know. I had it all worked out. She said she had the money we asked for hidden in a safe place and that she'd give it to us once we handed over our proof. I headed out to get it and when I came back she was dead. It was stupid of you to kill her before we completed the transaction."

"I didn't mean to kill her," Betty said. "I know the plan was just to blackmail her and then leave, but when I came into the kitchen and saw her in the pantry humming Donny's favorite Christmas carol I lost it."

He cleared his throat again. I remembered Jeremy saying the man who had been in the bakery on the night Candy died had cleared his throat constantly. Could the private detective have decided to use the proof he'd found to blackmail Candy rather than turn it over to the sheriff? It sounded like it.

"The pantry," he said. "Maybe we should take another look in the pantry."

Uh-oh. I slid down onto the floor from my sitting position. I closed my eyes and prayed he wouldn't come in to search.

"No! It's not in the pantry," Betty insisted. "I've searched the place from top to bottom. Let's just go. I told you I looked everywhere. If I haven't found the money by now we never will."

"How do I know you didn't find it and are now trying to execute some kind of double-cross?"

"You think I'd stick around if I was going to double-cross you? It's been a week. I looked everywhere. Trust me; if I'd found the money I would have split. Now we really should head out while we still can. The cops have been snooping around. I think they might be on to us."

The man grunted before they both left the kitchen.

Okay, now what? As odd as it seemed, I was almost willing to bet Betty hadn't told the PI I was in the pantry. I couldn't imagine why not, but I hadn't heard her say a word about me being hidden inside, and when he'd suggested searching the pantry she'd stopped him. Either she wanted to have the pleasure of killing me herself later or she didn't intend to kill me at all. I had no idea which was true, but I hoped it was the latter. Either way, I knew I needed to get out of there before the couple from hell came back.

I tried to loosen my arms, but the ropes had been tied securely. I moved back into a sitting position and considered my options. There were knives in the kitchen. If I could somehow make my way there I might be able to use one of them to cut the ropes around my wrists. Once I accomplished that I could free my feet and get the heck out of there. The problem was that I'd have to expose myself to do that, and if they came back and the PI really hadn't been aware I'd been tied up in the pantry, my standing in the kitchen with duct tape over my mouth would alert him to that fact pretty quick.

My other choice was to wait and hope they were gone for good. But I'd still risk exposure should the PI insist on searching the pantry instead. I could always try to wiggle my way out the back door and go to one of the nearby shops for help, but that would involve exposing my presence to anyone who might walk into the kitchen as well.

Finally, I decided I couldn't sit there a minute longer. I leaned on the wall behind me as I maneuvered myself into a standing position. Then I carefully hopped my way to the pantry door. It took a bit of doing, but I managed to turn around without falling and use my hands to open the door. I took a deep breath and hopped into the kitchen. I figured finding a knife was my best option, so I hopped over to the drawers located under the countertop and began to search for what I'd need.

I found a knife and had begun to work on the rope when I heard them returning. I slid down to the floor and hid under the counter. If they looked down they'd see me for sure; I just hoped they didn't.

"I think we should look in Candy's house again. The money obviously isn't in the bakery," Betty argued.

"Maybe not, but I'm going to have a look around myself before we head out."

"I told you, the cops are on to us. We should go now."

"It's Christmas Eve. I doubt anyone is going to come around with more questions until next week. I'm going to recheck the pantry."

I watched Betty's face as the PI opened the pantry door. Her look of alarm confirmed my suspicion that she hadn't told him I'd been tied up inside. When he began tossing things off the shelves she frowned and peered inside. I could see her looking around the room as soon as she realized I was no longer there. I wasn't sure if she'd seen me in the kitchen or not.

I knew it would only be a matter of time before the PI found me, but I wasn't sure what I could do to get away without him seeing me. He was in the pantry now, so if I was really quick…?

Betty opened the door to the alley. She glanced in my direction, then headed to the pantry. "Here, let me help you," she said.

I scooted out from under the counter, crawled to my feet, then hopped as fast as I could toward the open door.

"Who the hell are you?" the man asked before I could get halfway across the kitchen. I glanced at Betty, who begged me with her eyes not to rat her out.

I used my eyes to motion that I couldn't very well speak with tape covering my mouth. He told Betty to pull it off in one long motion.

"Ouch," I said as she ripped.

"Who are you?" he repeated.

"Zoe. And who are you?"

"Never mind about that. What are you doing in here?"

I looked down at my tied hands and feet. "This is sort of embarrassing, but my husband…well, he likes it kinky. I knew this shop was closed, so, well…" I pretended to blush.

"Yeah, like I'm buying that." He turned to look at Betty. "Do you know anything about this?"

"No. I swear," Betty answered.

"Why is it I don't believe you?" He grabbed Betty by the arm. I knew I was at that place where I had little to lose, so I opened my mouth and screamed as loud as I could. He balled up his fist and hit me. That, I'm afraid, led to my second nap of the morning.

When I finally came to, Zak was holding me in his arms. Salinger had both Betty and the PI in cuffs and was reading them their rights.

"God, Zoe, are you okay?"

I put my hand to my jaw. There was no doubt about it; I was going to have a bruise. "Yeah," I answered. "I'm okay. Where did you come from?"

"When you didn't answer your phone I came looking for you. I saw your car parked out front and had a feeling something was up when I realized you were parked in front of the bakery, so I called Salinger." Zak helped me to my feet. "I'm taking you to the hospital."

"No. Please. I'm fine. I just want to go home."

Zak looked uncertain.

"Please."

"Go ahead; take her home," Salinger said. "She was only out for a minute. Less than a minute. She's gonna have a bruise, but I think she'll be fine. I'll come by later to get her statement."

"Betty killed Candy," I blurted out. "And the PI tried to blackmail her."

Zak picked me up in his arms like I was a rag doll. "We can fill Salinger in later."

"Okay." I put my hand to my head. I really was going to have a headache. I rested against Zak's chest as he carried me out to the truck, where he gently set me on the seat.

"Are you sure you won't at least get checked out?"

"I'm fine. Really. If I start to feel not fine I'll let you know. I promise."

I could see Zak wasn't happy about my decision, but he started the truck without arguing.

"My car."

"We'll get it later."

"There are gifts. On the seat. Can you get them?"

Zak looked like he might argue, but instead he opened his door.

"And no peeking," I added as he climbed out of the truck. "Promise me."

"I promise."

Chapter 13

Despite the fact that the day had started out about as bad as a day can, it ended up pretty darn nice. Zak didn't want me going out after my ordeal, so my parents, my sister Harper, my grandfather, Hazel, Levi, and Ellie all came over to us.

Zak made a huge feast that we all devoured before settling in to exchanging presents.

"This is for you." Scooter stood in front of me holding a brightly wrapped gift.

I held out my arms, indicating that he should sit down on the sofa beside me. I hugged the boy with all my might. "Are you okay?" I asked.

Scooter nodded. His father had decided to allow him to continue to live with Zak and me at least for the rest of the school year. He was to spend every school break with his dad in L.A., as well as next summer. At the end of the summer it would be decided whether he was going to return to Ashton Falls for the school year or remain in L.A.

"Yeah. I'm fine. My dad is picking me up in a little while and I'm going to miss having Christmas morning with all of you, but he promised me he'll bring me back before school starts in two weeks."

"I think your dad came up with a good solution."

"I guess. Open your present."

I carefully folded back the festive paper to reveal a photo of Scooter and me that Zak had snapped the previous winter nestled inside a handmade frame. We were laughing as we rolled around in the snow after a very competitive snowball fight. I almost cried when

I saw our smiling faces, but when Scooter turned the photo over and showed me the inscription, I began to bawl.

It said: *For Zoe, the best mom a kid could ever have.*

"You don't like it?"

I hugged Scooter with all my might. "I love it."

"But you're crying."

"Happy tears. They're happy tears."

"I'm glad. I loved my real mom, but she's been gone a long time. Sometimes I have a hard time remembering her, but I know she'd be very happy I have you to take care of me."

I hugged Scooter again and cried until I was all cried out.

"That turned out to be a really nice evening," Zak said after everyone had left. We were sitting in the seating area of our bedroom in front of the fire. Zak had set up a small tree in the room that lent it a cozy feeling, "Ellie seemed to love her sweater."

"She did, but I suspect not as much as the ring she got from Levi. I can't believe they're getting married tomorrow."

"It does seem quick."

"I suppose. Although I think they've been leading up to this their whole lives. I'm glad Scooter's dad decided to wait to leave town until after the ceremony."

"Yeah. Me too." Zak kissed me on the head as I sat tucked under his arm.

"It was sweet of Scooter to agree to go back to the hotel with his dad tonight so they could be together on Christmas morning. It looked like it meant a lot to him."

"I agree." Zak tightened his arm around me. "We really do have ourselves a pretty great kid." Zak settled into the sofa. "I guess I should say *two* pretty great kids. It was so sweet of Alex to give you her story for Christmas."

"It really was." I felt like I was going to cry again. Phyllis had helped her to have it bound with a very professional-looking cover. I kissed Zak on the cheek and began to get up. "I have something for you."

Zak grinned. "Is it the same thing you gave me last Christmas Eve?"

I grinned back. "Okay, maybe I have two things for you tonight. I want you to open this first." I walked over to the tree, where I picked up a small package wrapped in red paper. I handed it to him and then sat back down next to him.

"Are you sure you want me to open this now? I feel like we should wait until tomorrow when the kids are here."

"This is most definitely not a kid-appropriate gift." I knelt down in front of Zak and handed him the package.

Zak grinned again. "Yeah?"

"Yeah."

I watched Zak's face as he opened the gift. His mouth fell open. "Is this what I think it is?"

I nodded as Zak stared at the pregnancy test kit.

"So are we pregnant?"

"I'm not sure. I have been feeling a little funky but I haven't done the test yet. I wanted us to find out together."

Zak set the kit aside. He placed his hands on my cheeks and looked me in the eye. "However this turns out I want you to know that I love you and pregnant or not I wouldn't have it any other way."

"That doesn't make sense."

"Sure it does. I want us to have a baby when the time is right. If that time is now I'm happy that the time has come, and if the time is not now, I'm happy we are waiting until it is."

Chapter 14

Sunday, December 25

The Wedding

I don't know how they did it, but somehow my überorganized mother teamed up with my überorganized husband and pulled off a beautiful wedding in less than twenty-four hours. Zak had even managed to have Coop, his pilot, fly Ellie's mother and Levi's mother and sister in for the ceremony.

"Everything is just perfect." Ellie beamed as she sipped club soda from a champagne flute. "I have to admit, though, that I'm kind of nervous."

"Why?"

"I guess when Levi stated quite emphatically that we were getting married today no matter what, I pictured a small affair with just you and Zak and Levi and me. There must be fifty people here."

"Yeah, well, you know my mother. She's definitely superwoman when it comes to party planning."

"She really is. How do I look?"

My eyes filled with tears. "Beautiful." Mom had a white velvet dress she'd altered to fit Ellie, who was about as beautiful a bride as I'd ever seen.

I looked around the room, surprised myself at how perfectly perfect everything looked. We'd decided to have the ceremony in our house, with only the addition of red and white roses to the Christmas decorations we already had. Phyllis and Hazel had pitched in to organize the food and Pastor Dan had left his family for an hour to marry Ellie and Levi.

All the people with whom Levi and Ellie shared their lives had taken a break from their own holiday celebrations to take part in their special day.

Tears filled my eyes as my dad walked Ellie down the aisle. Her face glowed with happiness as she met Levi's eyes. For the first time since she'd told me she was pregnant, I really believed everything would be okay.

"We are gathered together to unite this couple before God, family, and friends," Pastor Dan began.

I swore I wasn't going to cry, but of course I was a total mess before Pastor Dan got the first sentence out of his mouth. Zak took my hand in his and gave it a squeeze of support when the first tears started flowing. I suppose I could attribute the tears to pregnancy hormones, although I wasn't sure there were any to attribute them to. Zak and I had decided to wait to do the test until after the wedding because we didn't want the result to in any way influence our enjoyment of Ellie and Levi's special day. I wasn't even sure how I wanted it to work out. If I were really honest with myself, I think I equally hoped I was and wasn't pregnant. Zak seemed content to let nature set the pace, so I supposed I'd take a note from his book and do the same.

As Ellie vowed to love Levi for all her days and Levi vowed to do the same, I couldn't help but imagine the four of us growing old as our children grew up together, best friends for life. The idea of family holidays and vacations filled me with joy as I glanced at Alex and Scooter, who stood together holding hands, and prayed with all my heart that these special individuals would always be part of our lives.

"I now pronounce you man and wife," Pastor Dan concluded as every eye turned to the brand-new couple.

UP NEXT FROM
KATHI DALEY BOOKS

Bonus Short Stories

This novella was originally published as *Zimmerman Academy New Beginnings*. I'm sharing it with you again so those of you who haven't had the opportunity to do so can read it if you wish. I never plot ahead, but my instinct tells me things may become complicated for Phyllis, Will, and Ethan in the future, and these short stories set up the conflict. This special novella is divided into two sections. The first contains a reprint of the chapters from Phyllis's perspective, which were included in *Hopscotch Homicide*, *Ghostly Graveyard*, and *Santa Sleuth*. The second contains a newer short story that took place on Phyllis's birthday.

Phyllis's Diary

Welcoming the Girls
The First Day of School
The First Date
New Traditions
Our First Dinner Party
The First Kiss
The New Forty
The Birthday Mystery

Welcoming the Girls

Looking back, I knew in my gut that my life was about to change forever. As an intentionally isolated individual who had spent the past sixty-two years avoiding the complicated emotional entanglements that seem to come standard with interpersonal relationships, I found that I was a lot more nervous than I wanted to admit. I guess the first time I really let the effects of my actions sink in was the day the girls arrived. As I stood stoically in my living room, waiting for Armageddon to rain down, I felt the life I had built to that point slowly slipping away.

"Oh, lord, what have I done?" I asked my cat, Charlotte.

Charlotte wound her body around my legs in a circle eight pattern as I looked out the window. What made me think I could take responsibility for three teenage girls? Was I crazy?

Apparently.

When Zak talked to me about helping him with the Zimmerman Academy, I'm afraid I let sixty-two years of loneliness burst forth in an orgasmic eruption of helpfulness.

"Sure, I'd love to help you oversee development," I said aloud. "You want me to be the principal? It would be a dream come true. Help out with the teaching during this first year of transition?

Absolutely." I looked down at Charlotte. "Whatever was I thinking?"

Charlotte stopped her journey through my legs and jumped up onto the table next to where I was standing. She knew she was not allowed on the table, but she also knew I was so far into my tirade that I wouldn't pay her the least bit of attention.

"I know I didn't have to offer to lodge the girls," I admitted. "It just seemed to make sense at the time. We do have a lot of extra bedrooms in this big, empty house."

Charlotte greeted my rant with a yawn, followed by a look of derision.

"Fat lot of help you are." I sighed. "Do you think it's too late to back out?"

Charlotte rolled her eyes. Or at least I imagined she'd roll her eyes if cats could actually perform such a task.

I looked out the window to the yard I'd so painstakingly nurtured. It was a lot of work, but my flower garden gave me such a deep feeling of serenity and contentment. I'd always wanted a cottage-style house despite the fact that I'd settled in the mountains. When I'd first seen the large two-story structure, which was so different from the log houses that populated the area, I knew I'd found the home I'd always dreamed of. The garden hadn't grown up overnight. It had taken years of love and nurturing to coax the seedlings into large and healthy plants. Over the years I'd found that gardening in an alpine environment can be challenging at the least.

I turned away from the window and looked around the room. I decided the baby grand piano really could use a good dusting even though I'd dusted that morning. I thought about heading toward the cleaning supply closet to look for a dust cloth, but I realized the girls wouldn't care about imaginary dust. I glanced at the clock. It was seven minutes after four. Hadn't Zak said they'd be here at four?

Charlotte jumped from the table to the windowsill and meowed. I looked out the spotlessly clean window just in time to see the large white van as it rolled to the curb.

Just breathe.

I took one last look at the surgically clean room and turned toward Charlotte. "They're here. Are you ready?"

Charlotte took one look at the crew that was piling out of the van, jumped off the windowsill, and took off up the stairs.

Traitor.

I took a deep breath and looked down at the pencil skirt I'd worn with sensible shoes and a white silk blouse. If there was ever an outfit that was all wrong for meeting a group of teenage girls for the first time this was it.

God, Phyllis, you are such an old maid. They're going to hate you.

As Zak helped the girls unload their things, I looked in the hallway mirror and considered the woman I'd become. Where had the years gone? It seemed like only yesterday that Bobby Davenport had asked me out on the one and only date I'd ever been asked on. I'd had a crush on the guy for over a year and couldn't believe he had actually noticed me. I remember that it felt like I was swimming in a pool of desire and excitement when he smiled at me. Which is why I'd, quite illogically, turned him down.

I'd used the pretext of having a history exam to study for, but I knew in my heart that wasn't true. At the time I don't remember making a conscious decision *never* to date, fall in love, or marry. In that moment all I'd *really* decided was that I was too scared to go on *that* date. I remember wondering how I'd gotten to be an elderly twenty-one years old without ever having been kissed. Everyone else I knew was well versed in the art of lovemaking by the time they'd reached their third decade, but me? I'd buried my face in a book, ignored the world, and missed my one and only chance at normal.

I touched my hand to the slight wrinkling around my eyes. I hadn't even noticed that my skin had begun to sag. It felt as if it had happened in a heartbeat. One moment I was a young and vibrant academic with a bright future ahead of her and the next I was an old woman living with a cantankerous cat.

"It's never too late for a new beginning," I coached myself as I tucked a lock of gray hair into a serviceable bun. "No need to fret about what could, would, and should have been. Today I will turn the page and begin a new chapter."

I ran a hand over the surface of the spotless coffee table one last time before I headed to the front door and opened it wide.

"Zak, Zoe." I held out my arms to the couple I'd grown to care for deeply. "I'm so happy you finally made it."

"Sorry we're late," Zoe said as she hugged me as soon as she arrived at the front door. "The traffic was a bear."

"I can imagine it would be, given the holiday."

"Phyllis King, this is Eve, Pepper, and Brooklyn," Zoe introduced with enthusiasm.

I greeted each of the girls in turn.

Eve Lambert was tall and thin, with brown eyes and straight brown hair that hung to her shoulders. The youngest of the group at fourteen, she was shy yet polite and always seemed to say all the right things, but her inner light didn't quite reach her eyes. I knew in a minute that Eve was a younger version of myself. Her breeding was too engrained into her personality to allow her to appear bored even though it was obvious she *was* bored. I'm certain she was counting down the minutes until she could retire to her room and dive back into the book she was clutching in one hand.

Prudence "Pepper" Pepperton was a tiny little thing who reminded me a lot of Zoe. She had dark curly hair and blue eyes that danced when she spoke. Pepper was the middle "child" at fifteen. Based on the way she was jumping around with more energy and enthusiasm than could be contained in one body, I was confident in going out on a limb and thinking she was going to be the ice breaker and cheerleader of the group. When I was fifteen I would have found Pepper's enthusiasm exhausting, but now I found myself somewhat enchanted by the elflike girl who ruthlessly abused the English language as she talked a mile a minute about anything and everything.

Blond-haired, blue-eyed Brooklyn Banks was the girl I'd always secretly longed to be. At sixteen she was beautiful and sophisticated, with a natural confidence that stated to the world that she knew what she wanted and knew how to get it. I could never have pulled off the Brooklyn attitude when I was her age, even if I'd been half as beautiful as she. She too looked bored, but unlike Eve, who wanted to dive into a book, I suspected Brooklyn wanted to dive into the boyfriend she'd been forced to leave behind when she'd been kicked out of her last school for smoking in the dorm.

I stepped aside and invited everyone inside as Zoe competed with Pepper for airtime. Zak brought in the luggage as Pepper and Zoe talked a mile a minute, but to be honest, I wouldn't remember a thing either of them said. I smiled as was expected, and I'm sure I was able to string together comprehensible sentences, but I really couldn't remember ever being as nervous as I was at meeting the trio of young women I was about to share my life with.

"Let me show you to your rooms so you can get settled in before dinner," I offered after the luggage had been deposited in my entryway.

Suddenly my house felt full. I hadn't lived with anyone, other than a series of feline companions, since I'd moved out of my parents' house to attend college. I'd had a few opportunities along the way to share my life with a roommate, but I'd always liked the quiet. Not that I hadn't had friends. During my sixty-two years I've shared my life with many wonderful people. But in all that time, I've never shared my life with anyone who was really mine.

Zak and Zoe followed behind the girls as I escorted my new housemates to the rooms I had chosen for them. Each of the three bedrooms I'd selected was large and nicely decorated. Each room had both a bed and sitting area, and each had a private bath.

"I don't do pink," Brooklyn informed me when I opened the door to a bedroom with a pink duvet, pink curtains, and a white sofa.

"I like pink," Pepper offered.

"Very well, then, Pepper, this shall be your room," I decided.

Pepper trotted inside and jumped up on the bed, squealing in delight when she noticed the clawfoot tub in the corner. She hopped off the bed and ran across the room to the tub, which she immediately climbed into to check it out for a comfortable fit.

"Dinner will be at seven. I hope you like pork roast."

"I love all food," Pepper assured me.

I smiled and took a breath. One down, two to go.

Zak delivered Pepper's luggage to her room while Zoe, Brooklyn, and Eve followed me down the hall. I opened the door to the room I had at one time converted into an office and library but had since converted back into a bedroom. The conversion of the room was complete other than the fact that I hadn't had the opportunity to remove all the books from the shelves.

"Bookshelves." Eve gasped. "Lots and lots of bookshelves, packed with all these lovely books. Can this room be mine?"

Brooklyn shrugged. "Fine by me."

Eve walked directly over to the wall that was lined with dark cherry wood shelving. I'd seen the love in her eyes when she'd spotted my rare book collection. I felt some of the tension leave my body, only to return when Eve informed me that she was a vegetarian. I almost panicked until I realized I had both a salad and vegetables to go with the pork roast, as well as whole grain bread I'd picked up that morning from the bakery. My mind immediately turned to other vegetarian options. Perhaps I'd try the new recipe I'd recently found for spinach ravioli lasagna, or maybe even the eggplant casserole I'd recently tried at a friend's house. Two down and only one to go.

The last room was the largest of the three. It was nicely furnished and spacious, but the truly amazing thing about it was the walk-in closet with satin-lined drawers, shoe racks, and a rotating clothing rod. When I noticed Brooklyn's look of boredom turn into one of elation, I knew deep inside that things were going to be all right.

"Do you have any dietary restrictions?" I asked as Brooklyn twirled around in the middle of the huge closet.

"I don't eat carbs."

"No carbs. Got it. Is there anything else I should know?"

Brooklyn stopped twirling and looked at me. "I haven't had a mother for a very long time; I don't need mothering."

"Don't have a mother? But I just recently spoke to your mother."

"I didn't mean literally; I just mean that I'm sixteen and have lived away from home since I was very young. I've attended boarding school during the academic year and camp during the summer since I was six. I'm used to taking care of myself and making my own decisions."

"I see."

Brooklyn must have noticed my look of concern because she quickly followed up with, "Look, I'm not going to be a problem. I promise. It's actually very nice of you to allow me to stay here after I was kicked out of my old school. I just wanted to let you know that I don't need a lot of active parenting."

"All right," I said. "I can respect that, and as long as you follow the house rules and do well in your classes I'll try to give you some space."

"Awesome. I'm going to need to find a local doctor. Can you recommend one?"

"Are you ill?" I asked.

"Birth control."

"Oh." I know I blushed, which I found embarrassing; a woman of my age should be able to discuss birth control without turning red.

God, Phyllis, you are such a child.

After I assured Brooklyn I would get her a list of gynecologists in the area, I left the girls to unpack. Once I'd taken a few deep breaths to steady my pounding heart, I said my good-byes to Zak and Zoe and headed toward the kitchen to check on the meal I'd prepared. I like to cook but rarely do with only myself to feed. It would be nice to have mouths to feed on a regular basis, even if two of them had adopted restricted diets.

I rechecked the oven for what must have been the tenth time that day. The meat looked moist and tender, as I'd hoped it would be. Eve, I decided, was going to miss out on something wonderful.

I put the potatoes on to boil and decided to head into the formal dining room to set the table. I'm not certain why I'd purchased such a large table when I'd bought and furnished the house. I rarely entertained and certainly never fed enough people to even begin to fill each of the twelve hardwood chairs. I planned to set one end of the table to create a more intimate dining experience.

After wiping down the dust-free surface I turned toward the antique hutch I'd bought at an estate sale and considered which place settings to use. This was a special occasion. Perhaps I should use Mama's china. And then again, I didn't want to have the girls feeling awkward by making a fuss. Perhaps the everyday dishes would be fine.

"Can I help?" Pepper asked as she entered the room through the kitchen.

"I'm trying to decide which dishes to use for our dinner."

"Does it matter?"

"No," I admitted. "I suppose it doesn't." I held up two dinner plates. "Which shall it be?"

"The ivory with the small blue flowers."

"There are linens in that drawer behind you. Why don't you pick out some placemats and napkins and I'll fetch the silverware."

Pepper chatted about the food at the last school she'd attended while we worked together to set a beautiful table for our first meal together. When the table was ready she followed me into the kitchen, where she continued to ramble on about various subjects while I prepared the vegetables. Pepper informed me that she too liked to cook, which she proved by preparing a colorful salad while I saw to the beverages. I found I rather liked preparing a meal alongside another person.

"I really love your house," Pepper complimented. "When Mr. Zimmerman pulled up to the front and I saw those blue shutters and all those beautiful flowers I knew I was going to be happy here."

"I'm so glad you like it. I've always liked to garden. Perhaps you'd like to help me when you have some free time."

"I'd like that."

"Tell me about yourself," I urged.

"I'm not sure what there is to tell. My full name is Prudence Partridge Pepperton. It's a mouthful, I know. When I was a baby my nanny began calling me Pepper and it stuck. My father is the only one who ever calls me Prudence."

"And your mom?" I asked.

"She's dead. She committed suicide last winter, after my father left her for one of his creations."

I frowned. "Creations?"

"My father is a plastic surgeon in Beverly Hills."

"I see." Pepper's announcement didn't quite fit with her airy tone of voice. At first I thought she was pulling my leg, but the tension around her eyes said otherwise.

"I am so sorry," I replied. "I really had no idea. That must have been an incredibly difficult time for you."

Pepper shrugged. "Yeah. I guess."

She looked away, struggling, I think, to maintain her composure.

"And why did you decide to attend Zimmerman Academy?" I changed the subject.

"I didn't decide. My father did. He left my mom, and then he didn't want me."

"Oh, I'm sure that isn't true." I couldn't imagine a parent not wanting his child.

"No, it is," Pepper assured me in a very matter-of-fact tone. "When my mom told me that my dad had taken off with one of his creations, I thought there would be a messy custody battle over me, but my father sat me down and told me that he had a new wife and a new life and he thought I'd be better off staying with my mother. I thought he'd visit, but he never did."

I put my hand to my heart to try to keep it from breaking.

"After Mom died I had no choice but to go stay with my father," Pepper continued. "I thought he would be happy to see me, but I could tell I was cramping his style. He knows Mr. Zimmerman somehow, and when he found out about the Academy, he asked if I could attend as a boarder. Mr. Zimmerman said he was thrilled to have me, so here I am."

"Well, I am thrilled to have you as well." I offered her my warmest smile. "I think the five of us are going to have a wonderful time this year."

"Five of us?" Pepper asked.

"You and me, Brooklyn, Eve, and Charlotte."

"Charlotte? I haven't met her."

"Charlotte is my cat. She decided to hide, but I'm sure she'll make an appearance once she gets used to all the commotion."

Pepper smiled. "I always wanted a pet. My father isn't a fan of pet dander, so I was never allowed to have one. Do you think Charlotte would want to sleep with me?"

"Honestly," I replied, "probably not. She's an old cat and set in her ways."

Pepper's smile faded just a bit.

"But perhaps Zoe can find a younger cat for you. She runs a shelter, you know."

Pepper grinned. "Really? A cat of my own?"

"I can't promise that you'll be able to take it with you when you leave here, but as far as I'm concerned, the cat can be yours while you're here."

Was I crazy? Charlotte was going to have kittens. Not literally. She was too old for kittens, but I could guarantee she'd throw a diva kitty tantrum.

"Of course you must promise to take care of it," I added. "Having a pet of your own is a big responsibility."

Pepper ran across the room and wrapped her thin arms around my waist. She hugged me harder than I'd ever been hugged, and I felt my heart warm in a way it never had in all the years I'd resided on this planet. I hugged Pepper back and thanked the universe for the momentary insanity that had brought Pepper and the others into my life.

"I'll take care of all her needs. I promise," Pepper assured me.

I smiled. "It's late today, but we can call Zoe tomorrow to see what she has available."

Later that evening I decided to stop in to say good night to Eve. I'd actually managed to discover a fair amount of information about the other two girls, but Eve had been characteristically quiet for most of the evening. I felt that, more than any of the others, I understood Eve. I too was the type to use my words frugally when in a new social situation, but that didn't mean I didn't have anything to say or that I didn't want to feel included.

I knocked on Eve's door. The light was still on, so I knew she was still awake.

"Come in," she called.

I slowly opened the door. Eve was curled up in the big chair near the small wood stove with a book.

"I just wanted to say good night and to make sure you didn't need anything before I retire for the evening."

"Thank you. I'm fine."

I smiled. I really didn't know what else to say, so I began to close the door.

"I love your book collection," she added. "I hope it's okay that I borrowed one."

"Of course." I opened the door wider and stepped inside the room. "Please feel free to read anything you like. I was concerned at first that I should box them up because I was going to have boarders."

"Oh, no. Don't do that. Having a room filled with books is having a room filled with friends."

"I've always felt the same way. Not everyone understands the fact that many of the characters I've grown to love truly feel like people I know. What are you reading this evening?"

"*The Perks of Being a Wallflower.*"

"I haven't read that. Are you enjoying it?"

"I am. I actually just started it, but so far so good. What are you reading?"

Eve and I spent the next thirty minutes talking about my favorite subject: books. Although decades separated us in years, I found we'd read and enjoyed many of the same stories.

"I should be heading to bed," I said with a yawn. "I did want to ask if there was anything you needed, or anything I should know about you other than the fact that you're vegetarian."

Eve looked down at her book, but I could tell that she hadn't gone back to reading. "Not really."

"What made you decide to attend Zimmerman Academy?"

"I didn't decide. Attending the Academy was a deal that my court-appointed shrink and my public defender made with the district attorney to get me out of juvie."

I couldn't have been more shocked if she'd told me she had just arrived from an alien planet. I was beginning to regret my decision not to read the background information Zak had given me on each of the girls more thoroughly until after I met them. I didn't want to have what I read affect my first impressions of them.

"You were in juvie?"

"Yeah. I thought you knew."

"For what?"

"I put my stepdad in the hospital."

"Was it self-defense?" I had to ask.

"Not according to the judge. He said that adding sedatives to the scumbag's whiskey in the hope of rendering him unconscious didn't fall into the category of defending myself. It was the judge's opinion that I should have gone to an adult I trusted rather than taking action on my own. Of course to this point in my life I've never met an adult I trusted enough to share such a big secret."

I frowned. "Did your stepfather abuse you?"

"Every time he drank, and I have the scars to prove it." Eve stopped and looked at me. Her voice softened just a bit. "I didn't mean to actually hurt him; I just wanted to make him pass out. My friend gave me the idea to use the sedatives, so I tracked some down and began adding them to his whiskey. It really seemed to help. Every time he drank he'd fall asleep before he could get nasty. What I didn't know was that the drug I used builds up in your system over time, and he eventually overdosed. He's okay now and back at home, and I know I should feel bad about what I did, but all I actually feel is relieved that my plan succeeded in getting me out of the house."

I found that I was at a loss for words.

"Don't worry. I'm not dangerous," Eve promised me. "I just did a stupid thing."

"I'm not worried," I assured the girl. "I'm glad it worked out for you to come to Ashton Falls. You'll be safe here."

Eve looked down at her book again, but I felt as if we'd made a connection. At least I hoped we had. She, more than the others, seemed to need the kind of environment Zak and I hoped to provide at the Academy.

As I walked toward my room, I had to marvel at the set of circumstances that had landed me as housemother to a sexually active sixteen-year-old, an all-but-orphaned fifteen-year-old, and a fourteen-year-old client of the juvenile justice system.

I entered my room and began my nightly ritual. Charlotte curled up on my pillow as I began removing my makeup and moisturizing my skin. My mother, God rest her soul, had drilled into my head the importance of a proper cleansing and moisturizing ritual when I was still a young woman. She'd taught me a structured routine that I follow to this day.

"I will admit that the day has held its share of surprises," I began as Charlotte watched me go through the predictable steps of the process.

"Still, I have high hopes that the girls and I will do just fine. Pepper talks a mile a minute, so I know none of us will ever have to suffer the agony of awkward silence when she's around," I said aloud, confident that Charlotte actually was listening to my chatter.

"And, although Eve has a tragic past, I'm choosing to leave it in the past. You know, she really is quite interesting, and we like many of the same authors. She's read so many of the classics. I know we'll never lack for books to discuss."

I slipped a flannel nightgown over my head and then began sorting the clothes I had removed. I hung those that could be worn again on hangers and separated those that needed laundering into differing baskets for the laundry service.

"Brooklyn may prove to be a challenge in the long run," I informed Charlotte as I unwound my bun and began brushing my waist-length hair. "We'll have to see how things go. It is a bit odd that she's more experienced with boys and dating than I am. I hope I'll instinctively know how to handle any situations that may arise on that front."

After I brushed my hair one hundred times I fashioned it into a long braid that hung down my back.

"I think all the girls are both nervous and excited to begin classes next week. The transitional school Zak has organized for this year will accommodate ten students, five girls and five boys between the ages of twelve and sixteen, with the exception of Alex, who, as you know, is just ten. Three of them will be attending the middle school in the mornings and the other seven will attend the high school. Just the thought of high school fills me with terror, but I think our girls will do just fine."

Charlotte yawned. She appeared to be communicating that she had bored with my chatter. I ignored her.

"I find myself optimistic about the future. We're being offered not only the opportunity to spend more time with people we already love but the chance to bring wonderful new acquaintances into our lives as well."

I straightened the bathroom and headed back toward the sleeping area.

"Do you think I should dress up or down for my first day at the Academy?"

"Meow."

"Yes. That's what I thought as well."

After I was satisfied that I had done everything I needed to do to prepare myself for bed, I set to preparing the room. I worked my way around the area, straightening already perfectly straight books and knickknacks before opening my window just a quarter of an inch.

"I'm excited for the meet and greet Zak and Zoe are hosting tomorrow. I think it was such a good idea to provide an informal setting where everyone can get to know one another before classes begin. I would think that having an informal social event before the beginning of the school year will ease first-day jitters for students and staff alike. Of course most of the staff already know one another, but it will be nice to give Mr. Danner, the new teacher of mathematics, a chance to get to know everyone else. He's a widower, you know."

Charlotte tilted her head as she watched me.

"I know what you're thinking, but it's not true. I don't have a crush on Mr. Danner. Yes, he's very good-looking, and we seem to share a lot of interests in common, but he's five years younger than I am. Besides, his wife hasn't been gone all that long. I'm sure the last thing he's interested in doing is dating a sixty-two-year-old virgin."

Charlotte rolled over onto her back. I sat down on the side of the bed and gave her stomach a scratch as I pictured the new math teacher. He did have a nice smile, and the creases in the corners of his eyes turned upward, indicating that he smiled a lot. And really, if you think about it, a five-year age difference wasn't all that insurmountable once you passed the half-century mark.

"I'm just being a silly old woman." I stood up. "A man with Mr. Danner's looks and experience would never be interested in a dried-up old prune like me."

I set my ridiculous fantasies aside and continued with my nightly rituals. After stacking the extra pillows on my white tufted chaise, I poured myself a cup of tea from the warming pot I'd already brought up and added a splash of brandy. I then slid between my 1500-thread count sheets and settled in.

"Are you ready?"

Charlotte indicated that she was.

After placing my reading glasses on the tip of my nose, I adjusted the light and opened the hardcover book I'd chosen from the bookcase. Charlotte crawled into my lap and began to purr as I began to read aloud. Reading aloud to Charlotte was an activity we both enjoyed immensely, and it was a rare occasion when we missed this ritual at the end of the day. Tonight I'd chosen to once again begin the story of *Emma* by Jane Austin. Emma had spunk. I liked that.

Emma Woodhouse, handsome, clever, and rich, with a comfortable home and happy disposition, seemed to unite some of the best blessings of existence; and had lived nearly twenty-one years in the world with very little to distress or vex her.

I paused and contemplated the sentence. Could a life with little to vex or distress truly be a life worth living? I smiled as I continued with the story. I had a feeling that my controlled and efficient life was about to get a whole lot more complicated, and for the first time I realized that I couldn't wait to see how it all turned out.

The First Day of School

Having been involved in academia for most of my life, first as a student and then as a teacher, I've experienced the energy of the first day of school on many occasions. I will say that despite this familiarity with the rituals surrounding such an event, my first official day as a teacher at Zimmerman Academy was both as grand and as terrifying as any I had ever experienced. I have found that it is these seemingly routine events that, when captured in time, become the memories you cherish for a lifetime.

"What do you think?" I asked Charlotte.

"Meow."

I'd dressed conservatively in a shin-length gray skirt with a matching jacket and an ivory-colored blouse. By the look on Charlotte's face, she was more concerned about her breakfast than my attire. I studied my image in the full-length mirror. I doubted I'd win any beauty contests, but I'd done all right. I was certain the students wouldn't care if I showed up in a gunnysack, but I did want to look my best for my first day working with Mr. Danner.

I fluffed the pillows on the bed one last time as I looked around the room. Everything was in order, which meant that the only thing left was to head downstairs and face the girls. We'd settled into a comfortable companionship over the past few days, but I knew it was important not to let on how very nervous I actually was. Charlotte followed me down the stairs and into the kitchen, where she headed straight to her empty bowl.

"Salmon or tuna?" I held up two cans of the gourmet cat food I bought for Charlotte.

"Meow."

"Salmon it is." I forked the chunky meal from the can and into her dish. "I'm going to be away for a good part of the day today," I explained to my feline friend. "I know it makes you angry when you are left alone, but do try to behave yourself."

Charlotte ignored me, but I expected nothing more. I'd spoiled Charlotte horribly since she was a kitten, and the fact that she ruled the house was something we both understood as true.

I had turned my back to make a pot of coffee when I heard a hiss, followed by a growl. Annabelle must have decided to join us.

"Do you think Charlotte will ever like Annabelle?" a concerned-looking Pepper asked as she walked into the room with the small cat Zoe had helped us pick out.

"I'm not certain she will ever actually like her, but I'm sure she will grow to tolerate her," I answered honestly. "Your hair looks nice today."

"Thanks." Pepper fed Annabelle and then poured herself a glass of milk. "I wanted to do something fun for my first day. Should I make some eggs for us all?"

"Eve doesn't eat eggs," I reminded Pepper, "and Brooklyn doesn't eat breakfast, but I wouldn't mind some eggs if you are making some for yourself."

That earned me a huge grin. I found that Pepper was the easiest of the girls to understand and communicate with, and she seemed to really enjoy doing things for others.

"Did you enjoy your evening with Chad?" I asked. Chad and Pepper had really hit it off when they met at the meet and greet, and he had asked Pepper to attend a movie the previous evening. Because Chad's parents were going along I decided the outing would be harmless and encouraged her to go. I did so want the girls to have plenty of friends to ease the jitters I'd always associated with the first day at a new school.

"We had a really good time. Chad is superfunny, and he likes action flicks almost as much as I do. Mr. Carson invited me to go bowling with them on Thursday night. Would that be okay?"

"You like to bowl?" I asked as Pepper poured a bowl of beaten eggs into a hot pan.

"Sure. It's a lot of fun. I've only been a few times and I'm afraid I'm pretty bad at it, but Chad said he didn't care. He's going to give me some pointers. His family plays in the family league. Can you imagine being close enough to your family to bowl with them once a week?"

I couldn't, but it sounded nice.

"I'll speak to Chad's father, but as long as it is all right with him it is fine with me," I answered.

"You aren't going out with Chad again?" Brooklyn asked when she wandered into the kitchen just as our discussion was wrapping up.

"I am. Why?"

"He's just so…" Brooklyn paused as she poured herself a cup of coffee.

"Perky," Pepper supplied.

"Exactly."

"What's wrong with perky?" Pepper asked.

"It's exhausting. Chad talks more than you do. I really don't know how the two of you work out who'll talk when."

Pepper shrugged. "We manage."

"And bowling? Really? Since when is bowling an accepted pastime?"

"Don't be tiresome," I scolded Brooklyn. "Bowling may not be your cup of tea, but Pepper seems to enjoy it, so don't ruin it for her."

Brooklyn sighed. "You're right." She turned to Pepper. "I'm sorry. I tend to be bitchy before I've had at least two cups of coffee."

"Would you like some eggs?" Pepper held up the pan of eggs she was scrambling.

Brooklyn looked like she might vomit. I certainly hoped it wasn't too late for those birth control pills she'd requested.

"Is the flaxseed gone?" Eve asked when she joined us and began preparing a bowl of whole grain cereal, which I knew she'd top with fruit and soy milk.

"It may be," I answered. "Add it to the list and I will stop at the market this afternoon. If anyone else wants anything specific now would be the time to write it down."

"We're out of nonfat yogurt," Brooklyn commented.

"Add it to the list," I instructed.

"Is that what you're wearing today?" Brooklyn looked at me as she jotted yogurt on the list.

Suddenly I felt like a self-conscious child again as I looked down at my outfit. "I planned to."

Brooklyn frowned. "I don't mean to be rude, but don't you want to fit in?"

"Fit in?"

"To the twenty-first century. You have such nice features. Your hair is gorgeous, your skin is flawless, and you have an almost perfect facial ratio."

"Facial ratio?"

"You're a babe," Pepper supplied.

"You just need a little makeup and some less stodgy clothing and you'll have Mr. Danner drooling all over himself," Brooklyn declared.

"Mr. Danner? What makes you think I'm interested in Mr. Danner?"

All three girls rolled their eyes.

"How about it, girls?" Brooklyn asked. "Should we help Ms. King out?"

Pepper and Eve agreed they should.

"Oh, I don't know. I do have a certain reputation to uphold."

"Nonsense." Brooklyn took me by the arm as all three teenagers in my life escorted me back up the stairs. Brooklyn worked on my makeup and Eve took my hair down from its serviceable bun and brushed it out, while Pepper rummaged through my closet. The transformation from old maid to modern-day woman, amazingly enough, took only minutes.

"Wow," I said as I looked again in the full-length mirror.

My makeup was lightly yet expertly applied, my conservative skirt and blouse had been replaced by dress slacks and a soft cashmere sweater that made me look professional yet approachable, and the conservative bun I'd worn for most of my sixty-two years had been replaced by soft curls trailing down my back that had been pulled back in a large clip at the back of my neck. I looked at least ten years younger.

"Wow is right," Brooklyn agreed. "You look beautiful."

I smiled. "Thank you. All of you."

I could see the three teens were proud of what they had accomplished. It really was an amazing transformation. I almost didn't feel like myself.

"We'd better go," Eve said. "I wouldn't want to be late."

After Pepper and I made sure Charlotte and Annabelle were settled, the three girls and I gathered backpacks and supplies and headed out to the garage where I kept Lizzy, my 1955 Cadillac.

"You've heard about the hole in the ozone layer," Eve scolded as she surveyed the car my father left me.

"I am aware of the fragile nature of our environment and I don't often take Lizzy out for a spin, but my father used to take me to school in this car and I've taken myself to school in it on the first day of the new school year every year since he passed and left it to me. It is a tradition."

"Well, I love it." Pepper hopped into the front seat before any of the other girls had a chance to respond.

"It's a convertible," Brooklyn commented.

"Yes, dear. It is a nice morning, so I thought we'd arrive for our first day in style."

"I spent twenty minutes getting my hair just so. Riding in that thing is going to destroy everything I worked so hard to accomplish. Why can't we take your Volvo?"

"Because it is the first day of school," I insisted. "I always take Lizzy on the first day of school."

Brooklyn just looked at me.

"We can put the top up if that helps."

Brooklyn climbed into the backseat as I raised the top.

I looked at Eve, who was still staring at Lizzy like she was going to singlehandedly prove to be responsible for the downfall of mankind.

"It's just for today," I encouraged.

Eve shrugged and climbed in beside Brooklyn.

I slowly backed out of the driveway.

"So how exactly is this going to work?" Pepper asked.

"You will each attend classes at the public high school in the morning. I will pick you up after third period and we will all head into town, where Mr. Zimmerman has rented a building to temporarily house the Zimmerman Academy. Mr. Zimmerman, Mr. Danner, and I, along with some part-time staff, will provide additional classes catered to your individual needs."

"What about clubs and afterschool activities?" Brooklyn asked.

"We will try to accommodate any extracurricular activities you might have," I promised. "I know Dezil plans to join the football team. Is there something in particular you are interested in?"

"Nothing particular, but I like to keep my options open. You never know when a hot guy is going to ask you to hang."

"I want to be a cheerleader," Pepper stated.

"You'd be a wonderful cheerleader, with all your energy. I'm sure Mr. Denton can tell you how to go about trying out. How about you, Eve? Are there any afterschool activities you might be interested in?"

"I'd like to be on the school newspaper, if they have one."

"I'm certain they do. I believe there is a new staff adviser this year. Be sure to ask about it when you pick up your schedule."

I pulled into the parking lot. Normally, I'd just be dropping the girls off, but I wanted to be certain they received their class schedules without any problems, so I pulled into a parking space.

"You don't need to come in," Brooklyn announced when she realized I was parking.

"Are you sure?"

"We're sure," Eve answered.

Pepper opened the passenger side door and the three girls climbed out.

"We'll meet you in front of the school after third period," Brooklyn declared, slamming the door behind her.

I watched as the girls walked toward the entrance. I hoped they'd have wonderful first days. They seemed so confident and unaffected by their new situation. I was nervous for them, but they didn't seem nervous at all. I realized I could learn something from these remarkable young women.

After I dropped the girls off I continued on to the building that would house the Academy temporarily. Zak, Will, and I planned to have a staff meeting to discuss the division of labor for the first few weeks of school. Zak was going to teach a seminar in technology, Will planned to teach several accelerated math classes, and I was to handle literature and composition. While all of the students would be scheduled into all of the core subjects in any given week, Zak wanted to tailor each student's curriculum to their own interests and needs.

Pi, Dezil, Abby, Dex, and Hacker had been admitted to the program based primarily on their strength in the area of technology, while Alex, Brooklyn, Pepper, Eve, and Chad showed overall intelligence in a number of subjects. Both Alex and Eve shared my love of literature and writing, so my plan was to spend extra time with the two of them in that area.

I took a deep breath after pulling up in front of the Academy. It was one thing to let the girls "sex me up," but it was another to walk into a building where two of my male peers were waiting. Suddenly I was very sorry Zoe had been otherwise detained. Another female to divert the attention from the sweater I was suddenly convinced hugged my body much too snuggly would have been welcome indeed.

No guts, no glory, I whispered to myself.

I opened the door and prepared to exit Lizzy.

"This your car?" Will Danner suddenly appeared beside me.

"Yes. This is Lizzy."

This is Lizzy? Smooth, Phyllis

"She's really fantastic. I love old cars, especially old Caddies. Are you the original owner?"

"My father was."

Will ran his hand slowly over the fender, as if he were making love to it.

I felt my heart beat in my chest as I imagined his hand doing that to my body.

"I'd be happy to let you drive her if you'd like," I offered. "After the meeting of course."

Will's face lit up. "Really? I'd love to take her for a spin. But maybe when we have more time to really take a drive. Are you free on Saturday?"

Was I free on Saturday? Now there was a loaded question if ever I'd heard one.

I knew I should say no. I was nothing more than a silly old woman with a crush on a younger man. Whatever was I thinking?

"I believe I am free on Saturday," I found myself saying, almost against my will.

"Excellent. We can drive around the lake. I'll bring a picnic. I found this awesome little spot near some seasonal falls the last time I was visiting the area. They'll be little more than a trickle at this time of year but still beautiful."

"Sounds nice."

"Wear something casual. Shorts or jeans. And sturdy shoes. We might want to do some hiking."

Shorts or jeans? I was going to need to go shopping.

"It's been quite a day," I said to Charlotte later that evening as I prepared for bed.

"All of the girls seemed to enjoy their first day of school." I massaged night cream into my skin after I'd washed off the makeup Brooklyn had applied that morning.

"It looks as if Eve is going to be welcome on the newspaper staff, and it seems Levi managed to pull some strings to get Pepper included on the cheerleading team." I slipped a flannel nightgown over my head and then began sorting the clothes I had removed.

"It seems Chad is a cheerleader. I don't remember them having male cheerleaders when I was in school, but I guess it is now all the rage to have a coed squad."

Charlotte didn't say anything, but I could tell she was bored with my chatter.

"I wonder if I should ask the girls to help me get ready every morning. I have to admit their effort with my appearance had quite an impact, judging by the number of compliments I received today."

Charlotte continued to ignore me. The ungrateful beast.

"I've decided to make more of an effort with my appearance. I even stopped by that boutique Zoe assured me carries the best-quality cosmetics and stocked up on everything I might need."

Charlotte jumped up onto the counter in an effort to get my attention. I shooed her down.

"I couldn't help but notice Mr. Danner noticing me today." I smeared a nourishing balm onto my lips. "I even have a date with him on Saturday."

Charlotte swatted at the hem of my nightgown.

"I know what you are thinking," I added after I had decided I had done all I could with my face and removed the scarf from my hair.

"You think I am getting ahead of myself." I began the first of my one hundred brush strokes. "You think Mr. Danner was simply being cordial today when he asked to sit with me during lunch, and he was just being neighborly when he asked me out on a picnic on Saturday."

Charlotte yawned.

"I know you are probably right, but it's nice to feel like someone—anyone—might notice how nice I looked. It's been such a long time since I have felt like anything other than a stodgy old maid."

I finished brushing my hair and began to braid it. "I agreed to house the girls because I believed I could help them, but so far it seems it is they who are helping me. I can't remember the last time I've felt this alive. Between you and me, I actually felt visible today."

Charlotte rolled over onto her back in a feeble attempt to divert my attention away from my monologue.

I ignored her.

"I won't go so far as to say desirable. Oh, hell, I *will* say desirable. Today, for the first time in at least forty years, I felt desirable. Is that sinful of me?"

Charlotte rolled back over and meowed. She looked at me as if I'd lost my mind, then trotted out of the bathroom and into the adjoining bedroom.

"What would you know? You're a cat."

I followed Charlotte into my bedroom and began the task of straightening already perfectly straight books and knickknacks before opening my window just a quarter of an inch.

"I wonder if I should invite Mr. Danner to attend Sunday supper," I asked Charlotte as I stacked the extra pillows on my white tufted chaise.

"He did ask me to join him on Saturday, so I would simply be returning the invitation. It's the polite thing to do. Besides, he is new in town, and I imagine he would welcome a home-cooked meal."

Charlotte jumped up onto the bed.

"It wouldn't be as if I were asking him on a date. I mean, the girls will be here. No, it most definitely won't be a date, any more than our drive on Saturday is a date." I poured myself a cup of tea from the warming pot I'd brought up, then added a splash of brandy.

"I wonder if Mr. Danner would enjoy a nice roast beef with roasted vegetables. My mother taught me how to make a delicious roast with carrots and potatoes."

I squeezed a dollop of creamy lotion onto my hands and rubbed gently.

"And it has been a while since I had the occasion to make a chocolate cake. Men enjoy chocolate cakes. I know that for a fact," I informed Charlotte before I slid between my 1500-thread count sheets and settled in.

"Are you ready?"

Charlotte indicated that she was.

After placing my reading glasses on the tip of my nose, I adjusted the light and opened the hardcover book I'd chosen from the bookcase. Charlotte crawled into my lap and began to purr as I began to read aloud. Tonight we were reading *Jane Eyre* by Charlotte Brontë. I opened the book to the bookmark. I was about to begin when Charlotte swatted at the page, causing it to turn. I decided to begin at that point. I had read the book so many times it didn't really matter. That's the thing about favorite novels; they become a part of your history as much as anything else you experience becomes a part of your history.

It does good to no woman to be flattered [by a man] who does not intend to marry her; and it is madness in all women to let a secret love kindle within them, which, if unreturned and unknown, must devour the life that feeds it; and, if discovered and responded to, must lead, ignis-fatuus-like, into miry wilds whence there is no extrication.

"Are you trying to tell me something?" I asked Charlotte.

Charlotte began to purr.

"I'm not looking to marry Mr. Danner."

Charlotte tucked her head up under my chin. She often did this, I imagine, as a gesture of apology.

"You really are the most opinionated cat." I set the book aside and gathered Charlotte into my arms. "But I love you. Don't worry; your spot next to me in this bed is safe. I'm really nothing more than a silly old woman with schoolgirl fantasies."

The First Date

How is it that a person can live to the ripe old age of sixty-two before having a first date? Am I crazy to believe that perhaps it is not too late for such things? I suppose there comes a point when your time has passed and you should simply accept what life has served as the only offerings you are destined to sample. Not that I am complaining. I've lived a full life. A purposeful life. My time on this earth has not been wasted. Still, there are times I wonder at the things that might have been.

"Oh, my." I stood sideways in front of my full-length mirror and considered my rear. The girls had helped me pick out a pair of jeans—the first I've ever owned—for my picnic with Mr. Danner. When I'd tried them on in the store the lighting had been dim, so I hadn't realized how truly form-fitting they were.

"I don't think I can wear these," I said to Charlotte.

My diva cat yawned and then rolled over, a clear indication that she didn't care about my jeans or my rear.

I pulled the bright plum tank top the girls had selected for me over my head and then layered it with the matching cardigan I had insisted on. The sweater hung down to my hips, providing a bit of a barrier between my denim-clad sit-upon and the general public's judging eyes.

"I just don't know," I debated. I turned to Charlotte. "What do you think?"

Charlotte hopped off the bed and headed toward the doorway.

The ingrate.

I opened the door to release my traitor of a beast at the same time Pepper was walking past on her way toward the study, where the girls were watching television.

"Wow," she said. "You look great. And so different."

"Different good or different bad?" I wondered.

"Definitely different good. You look young and carefree and approachable."

"I don't normally look approachable?" I asked.

Pepper screwed up her face. I could tell she didn't want to hurt my feelings, but she didn't want to lie either.

She grabbed my hand and pulled me into the hallway. "Let's show the others."

Part of me wanted to retreat to my room and slip into a pair of sturdy wool slacks and a proper dress blouse, but the rest wanted to see what the others thought, so I let Pepper pull me down the hall and into the study, where Brooklyn and Eve were watching a reality show.

"So what do you think?" Pepper asked after she'd escorted me into the room.

"Wow, you look great," Brooklyn answered right away. I liked the fact that she didn't have to take her time to come up with a reply. It made her compliment seem more sincere.

"You really do look great," Eve added. "Those jeans fit you perfectly."

"Are you sure they aren't too tight?"

"Tight?" Brooklyn said. "If anything, they're a little loose, but you wanted the relaxed-fit jeans, so relaxed fit is what we got."

"And the color of the tank and sweater set matches your complexion perfectly," Eve added. "You look beautiful, although we'll need to do something about your hair."

"What's wrong with my hair?" I put a hand to my long locks, which I'd braided down my back.

"You're going driving in a convertible, so you had the right idea with the braid, but we need to do something softer like a French braid," Pepper mused.

"Maybe a fishtail," Brooklyn suggested.

"A fishtail?" I asked.

"Or a loose five strand," Pepper said with enthusiasm.

I looked at Eve. She nodded her agreement.

"Okay, I guess we can try a fishtail or a five strand," I said with caution.

"And your makeup. It's all wrong." Brooklyn got up from her chair. She clicked off the television. "Come with me and we'll get you fixed up."

Brooklyn took my hand and led me back down the hall to my bedroom.

"I did it the way you showed me," I complained as she sat me down in front of my vanity.

"You did it the way I showed you to do it for work," Brooklyn corrected. "You need something brighter for a picnic with your special guy."

"Mr. Danner is not my special guy," I countered. "He is simply a man with whom I work who shares a similar interest in classic cars."

All three girls rolled their eyes.

"This really isn't a date," I tried once again.

Brooklyn ignored my statement and began sorting through my makeup case. "Do you have mauve?"

"Mauve what?" I asked.

"Eyeshadow."

"No. Only the gray and the taupe."

Brooklyn stood up from her squatting position. "I have mauve. What time will Mr. Danner be here?"

"At eleven."

Brooklyn looked at the others. "That should be enough time, but we'll need to hurry. You guys get started on the hair and I'll run to my room and get the supplies we'll need."

Supplies? Who knew a casual drive followed by a completely platonic picnic could require so much preparation? Brooklyn fixed my makeup while Pepper and Eve fixed my hair. By the time Will showed up thirty minutes later I'd been assured by all three girls that I looked the bomb.

"Right on time," I greeted Mr. Danner upon opening my front door.

He was dressed in faded jeans, a Serenity High School sweatshirt, and newer-looking running shoes.

"You look nice," Mr. Danner complimented. "Is that a new sweater?"

"It is. I'm glad you like it." I blushed.

"Purple is one of my favorite colors. Are you ready?"

"I am. Come on in. I'll just say good-bye to the girls and then we can be on our way. It's such a lovely day for a drive. In fact, I can't remember when the weather has been more perfect."

"I have the things we'll need for our picnic in my car. Should I grab them now?" Mr. Danner asked.

"We can drive around to the front and transfer everything once we get Lizzy. Did you think to bring a blanket? It is always a good idea to bring a blanket."

"Who said old dogs can't learn new tricks?" I said to Charlotte that evening as I prepared for bed. "I wore jeans for the first time, I pulled off a five-strand braid, and after all these years, I finally went on a date. Sort of," I qualified as I gently wiped the makeup from my face with a gentle cleanser.

"I mean, it wasn't *really* a date. Even I know that. Mr. Danner's wife has only been gone for a year and he is still in mourning. But it felt like a date from where I was sitting. He picked me up at my door even though we took my car. He drove, and when we arrived at the falls he opened my door. He even took my hand as we crossed the rocks to the spot he had picked out for us to dine."

Charlotte jumped up onto the counter.

"I know what you're thinking. You're thinking he took my hand because he was concerned that someone of my advanced age might slip and break an ankle. But it wasn't like that. It was more a gesture of chivalry than an attempt to prevent an old lady from falling."

Charlotte batted my tube of eyeliner onto the floor, then pounced on it from her vantage point on the counter.

"I'm not a lovesick teenager. I realize that what Mr. Danner and I have, and most likely all we'll ever have, is a friendship. But it was still nice to have someone make an effort to see to my needs."

I patted my face dry, then added a thick and moist night cream.

"Did you know that, although Mr. Danner is a professor of theoretical mathematics, he has read most of the classics? And his knowledge of historical events is really quite exhaustive. It seemed obvious to me as we spoke that the man has enjoyed a well-rounded education. That's so important. Don't you think?"

I pulled my flannel nightgown over my head and then sat down to unbraid my hair.

"I find that I am very much looking forward to getting to know the man better. I asked Mr. Danner if he would like to join us for Sunday supper, but he said he had other plans for tomorrow."

Charlotte decided to attack my feet, in an attempt, I am sure, to get my attention and hurry me up.

"Stop that, you silly cat. I'll be ready when I'm ready. You know I need to brush and then braid my hair."

Charlotte gave up and headed into the bedroom.

I fixed my hair and followed her.

"If you had stayed and let me finish, you would have heard me tell you that, although Mr. Danner can't come to supper this Sunday, he did say that he would love to come on another evening. Perhaps the following week."

I shooed Charlotte off the bed so I could remove the pillows and set them aside. I opened the window a quarter of an inch, then went to the bookshelf to pick out the story we would share that evening.

"Perhaps we should shake things up a bit. We've been reading the classics, but how about a romance? A steamy romance."

"Meow."

"Oh, not too steamy."

I continued to thumb through the books on the shelf. There were so many wonderful choices, it was hard to pick just one.

"How about *A Rose in Winter* by Kathleen Woodiwiss?"

Charlotte began to purr, and I took that as consent.

"Tonight we will begin at the beginning," I informed Charlotte before I poured myself a cup of tea with a splash of brandy.

"This really is one of my favorites," I said as I slid between my 1500-thread count sheets and settled in.

"Are you ready?"

Charlotte indicated that she was.

After placing my reading glasses on the edge of my nose, I adjusted the light and opened the book. Charlotte crawled into my lap and began to purr as I began to read aloud from the introduction by Kathleen Woodiwiss.

"A crimson bloom in winter's snow,
Born out of time, like a maiden's woe,
Spawned in a season when the chill winds blow."

I paused and looked at Charlotte. "It's so nice to begin with a poem."

Charlotte purred all the louder.

"And it is so romantic."

I touched my hand to my lips.

"When we arrived back at the house Mr. Danner leaned over, and I thought he might kiss me," I confessed.

Charlotte patted my cheek with her paw.

"Of course he was only leaning over to grab his wallet, which he'd left in the glove box. Still, in that moment I thought that I might let him, should he try."

I set the book aside and gathered Charlotte to my chest. Maybe one day my lips would know the touch of another's, but that day was not today. I let the steady rhythm of Charlotte's purr soothe my soul as I ran my hands through her thick fur. The love of a cat might not be the same as the love of a man, but for today it was enough.

New Traditions

I have experienced many firsts since Brooklyn, Eve, and Pepper came to live with me. In many ways, I feel as if I am beginning a new chapter in my life at the ripe old age of sixty-two. In the past six weeks I have shared a home with someone other than my parents for the first time, gone on my first date, purchased and worn my first pair of jeans, and learned how to style my hair and apply makeup to bring out my best features. The first I am the most excited about, however, is sharing my first holiday with my new family. In the past I've never much bothered with the trappings associated with Halloween, or any other holiday, for that matter, but this year I want to establish new traditions and experience everything the season has to offer.

"Jeremy is here," Pepper called from downstairs.

"I'll be right down," I called back.

Jeremy Fisher is the assistant to my good friend Zoe Donovan. When I found out that he was going to be a single dad, I offered to let him rent one of the townhomes I own at a very reasonable price. At the time I thought I was doing the young man and his adorable daughter a favor, but Jeremy has allowed me to serve as a surrogate grandma to Morgan Rose, which has turned out to be a blessing without measure.

The girls absolutely adore Morgan, who is now eighteen months old, and she in turn adores them.

Today we are babysitting Morgan while Jeremy is busy with his band. They are playing a concert in the park, which the girls and I plan to attend after we take Morgan shopping for her Halloween costume. The girls and I will be looking for costumes as well because we are all invited to a party at Zak and Zoe's home on Halloween night. As odd as it may sound, this will be my first Halloween costume ever.

"P'ma," Morgan greeted me as I walked into the room. When Morgan began to talk I couldn't decide what to have her call me. I wasn't her actual grandmother, so Grandma seemed presumptuous, but Phyllis, Ms. King, or Professor all seemed wrong as well. P'ma, an amalgamation of Phyllis and grandma, is the name we came up with after trial and error.

"How's my girl?" I asked as Morgan reached for me and I took her into my arms. Morgan is an adorable child with dark brown hair and huge brown eyes. The lashes that framed her eyes were long and thick.

"Kitty," Morgan said after she planted a wet kiss on my cheek.

"The kitty is upstairs," I answered. Surprisingly, my cat Charlotte, who doesn't like anyone, likes Morgan, and the two have formed a bond that I have to admit I don't completely understand.

"Cookie?" Morgan tried instead.

"How about if Pepper gets you a cookie while I talk to Daddy?" I set Morgan on the floor. "Be sure to put a bib on her so she doesn't get the cookie all over her pretty pink jumper."

"I will," Pepper assured me as she took Morgan's hand and led her into the kitchen, where I kept a supply of cookies made especially for toddlers.

"I really appreciate your doing this," Jeremy said.

"You know I love to spend the day with Morgan as often as I can," I answered. "The girls and I are going to do some shopping and then we will see you at the park. Did you have a specific theme in mind for Morgan's costume?"

"Whatever you decide will be fine. I'm just happy for the help. Zoe has been superbusy lately, which means she hasn't been spending much time at the Zoo, which translates into Tiffany and me putting in extra hours."

Tiffany Middleton was Zoe's other full-time employee besides Jeremy, who was actually the manager of the facility.

"Maybe Zoe should consider hiring some extra help," I suggested.

"We've talked about it, but she seems to think that once things settle down a bit she'll have more time to spend with the animals. The problem is that Zoe seems to have a knack for getting involved. In *everything*. I really don't see her freeing up much time in the near future, although it does slow down at the Zoo over the winter, after the bears go into hibernation and the snow discourages pets from wandering too far away from home. I think we'll be fine until spring."

"I know Zoe wants what is best for the animals, so if you do find you need extra help I definitely think you should bring it up again."

"I will." Jeremy looked at his watch. "I really should get going. I'll see you at the park. Have fun shopping."

Jeremy left and I headed toward the kitchen, where I could hear Pepper and Morgan laughing. Of the three young women who have come to live with me, Pepper is the most outgoing. Pepper is a fourteen-year-old with a kind heart and a whole lot of energy. She is also by far the least complicated and easiest to get along with of the three, an extreme extrovert who would generate enough energy to power a small town if we could figure out a way to harvest it.

I had to smile as I observed Pepper chatting with Morgan, who sat contentedly in her high chair with cookie smeared all over her face. The pair seemed to be having a good time, so I decided to head back upstairs to finish getting ready.

"Can we stop off at the health food store while we're in town?" Fifteen-year-old Eve asked as I passed her on the stairs.

"Absolutely. We can make any stops you girls want."

"Thanks. We're out of flax seed and granola. I meant to add them to the shopping list, but I forgot. We could probably use some more fruit and veggies for my shakes too, if we have time to go by the farmers market, and I overheard Brooklyn saying we were getting low on coffee."

"Not a problem. We'll pick everything up while we are out."

Eve is not only a vegetarian and a health food nut but she is an introvert like I am. She loves to read and I suspect she is secretly trying her hand at writing as well. In spite of the five-year age difference between them, she has a lot in common with Alex, and the two spend a lot of time working on a project neither of them seems willing to share. I asked Zoe about it, but she said Alex is being as secretive as Eve. If I didn't know the two girls so well I'd be worried, but if there was anyone you could trust to do the right thing it was Alex.

After I finished applying my makeup the way the girls had shown me, I braided my hair and grabbed the new leather jacket I'd splurged on. It is a deep caramel color that perfectly matches the leather boots I'd also decided to buy. I had to admit the jacket spoke to a wild side I never even knew I had.

I said good-bye to Charlotte and headed down the hall to knock on Brooklyn's door. She is a sixteen-year-old with a troubled past who I was certain I'd never be able to handle, but as it turns out, she is an agreeable girl with a willingness to take on the role of big sister to the others. We haven't discussed her need for the birth control pills she mentioned on her first day with me, but I do know she has been to the doctor in spite of the fact that she doesn't appear to have a steady boyfriend.

"Come in," Brooklyn called.

I opened the door halfway. "I just wanted to let you know we will be heading into town in a few minutes."

"Does this top make me look fat?"

"Fat?" I asked. Brooklyn watches her weight more religiously than anyone I've ever met. "I doubt any top could do that, but in answer to your question, the sweater is adorable and it absolutely does not make you look fat."

Brooklyn smiled. "Good. Pi said we might hang after the concert and I want to look my best."

"You look beautiful as always and I love that deep blue color on you. It accentuates your blond hair and blue eyes. You look just perfect, although you might want to grab a jacket if you plan to go out after the concert. The temperature here drops dramatically after the sun sets."

Brooklyn sighed as she opened her closet and looked at the options. "I need something new. Something different. Like the jacket you're wearing. It's the bomb, by the way."

Brooklyn was a diva who usually thinks my clothes need updating, so it tickled me to death that she actually wanted a jacket like minc.

"You can borrow it if you'd like," I offered.

Brooklyn grinned. "Really? You wouldn't mind?"

"Not at all." Secretly, I was thrilled that young, sophisticated Brooklyn would want to borrow *anything* of mine.

"That would be awesome. I'll take really good care of it. I promise."

I handed the garment to the teenager. "I know you will. We leave in fifteen minutes. I'll meet you downstairs."

After I checked in on Pepper and Morgan, I headed out to the garage to warm up the car. Today we would take the Volvo because we have Morgan with us, but on most weekends I prefer the Caddy convertible my daddy left to me. There is something about cruising along the highway with the radio blaring and the wind in your hair that frees up your inhibitions.

I've been giving a lot of thought to the costume I will look for. On one hand, I wouldn't feel comfortable with anything too extravagant or revealing. Brooklyn mentioned her intention to dress as Cleopatra, which I'm most certain she can pull off in spite of her blond hair, but I think a sixty-two-year-old virgin should dress a bit more conservatively despite the fact that I've watched my diet and still wear the same size I wore in high school.

On the other hand, I don't want to go as anything too stodgy and conservative. Will Danner will be attending the party and I want to make an impression. The right impression. Pepper isn't sure what she wants to be and Eve plans to attend as Eliza Doolittle, the character from *My Fair Lady* and not the singer the girls like to listen to. I've been toying with a character from fiction myself. Finding just the right persona to adequately convey the image I'd like for Will to see has been more vexing than I imagined it would be.

I realize Mr. Danner will most certainly never look at me in quite the same way I look at him, but in spite of what Charlotte thinks, I feel there is no harm in giving my imagination just a bit of free rein. I've never met anyone quite like him. His personality is the perfect blend of archetypes melding the hero, the rebel, and the caregiver. Will is a caring man, a talented teacher, and a lively friend. His real gift, however, seems to be that of a magician because he is more than adept at making an old woman like me feel young again.

Pepper walked up behind me with Morgan in her arms. "Do you need help with Morgan's car seat?"

"It's in the trunk from the last time. I just need to strap it in."

"I'll do it," Pepper offered. "I wouldn't want you to hurt your back."

So much for feeling young.

Later that night, after we'd all returned home, I said my good nights, then headed upstairs for a little one-on-one time with Charlotte. We really had had the best day. We had all managed to find costumes we were happy with and Pepper bought a whole cartful of decorations to spruce up the house. Pepper and Eve were stringing lights around the windows when I decided I'd had enough fun for the day and was ready to come upstairs. Brooklyn had helped in the beginning, until Pi called, and she'd been in her room on the phone ever since.

I like Pi and am happy Brooklyn is interested in him, but I sense he might not return Brooklyn's affection to the same degree. He seems to be more interested in his music than dating, which, I suppose, isn't really all that odd when a young man is just sixteen.

Charlotte curled up on my pillow as I began removing my makeup and moisturizing my skin.

"You should see the costume we got for Morgan," I said to her as she watched me go through the predictable steps of the process. "It's a fuzzy lion that just makes me want to cuddle her up even more than I usually do. It was so cute the way she toddled around the costume shop, growling at everyone. I am finding that I do regret my decision not to have children of my own. I really did miss so much."

Charlotte yawned. It was part of my nightly routine to recount my day to her, but most of the time it appeared as if she wasn't really listening.

"Still, what is done is done and all I can really do is to cherish every minute I have with my adopted family. I am so very excited about Halloween for the first time in my life. Shopping with the girls was so much fun, and Morgan warms my heart every time I'm with her."

I slipped a flannel nightgown over my head and then began sorting the clothes I had removed. I hung those that could be worn again on hangers and separated those that needed laundering into differing baskets for the laundry service.

"We ran into Mr. Danner at the concert," I informed Charlotte as I unwound my bun and began brushing my waist-length hair. "I know we are just friends, and I know that is all we will most likely ever be, but I have to confess the man has a way of making my heart pound and my mood soar."

After I brushed my hair one hundred times I fashioned it into a long braid that hung down my back.

"I know you think I am being a foolish old woman to allow my mind to wander when it comes to thoughts of Will. And I know you are right. But a little fantasy of the romantic kind isn't really all that scandalous." Charlotte jumped off the bed and trotted across the room to the windowsill. She turned her back to me, effectively communicating that she was bored with my chatter.

"I know you tire of hearing about Will but there is no need to be rude."

Charlotte flicked her tail as I straightened the bathroom and headed back into my room.

"Do you think I should ask Will to supper this week? It does seem as if he has enjoyed the meals I have made for him. He still talks about the roast I made that first time he dined with us."

"Meow." Charlotte was still looking out the window. She probably just saw a squirrel and was meowing at it, but I chose to believe she was agreeing with me.

"Yes. That's what I thought as well. It is only neighborly to extend a hand of hospitality to the man. He is after all new to the area, and he hasn't had time to make a lot of friends."

Even as I said this I knew it wasn't true. Will was a friendly man who had made many friends during the short time he has lived in Ashton Falls.

After I was satisfied that I had done everything I needed to do to prepare myself for bed, I set to preparing the room. I worked my way around the area, straightening already perfectly straight books and knickknacks before opening my window just a quarter of an inch.

"Jeremy invited the girls and me to go trick-or-treating with him and Morgan before Zak and Zoe's party on Saturday. I believe he is going with Hank, Madison, and Harper," I said, referring to Zoe's parents and sister. "He said it's a tradition they began last year and would like to continue as the girls get older."

Charlotte tilted her head as she watched me.

"I've been thinking a lot about traditions now that I have the girls in my life. I'd very much like to establish some new ones with them. Costume shopping was a start, and decorating the house has been fun. Zak and Zoe have their big Halloween bash every year, so I suppose attending can become another tradition. I would like something special that is just ours, though."

Charlotte rolled over onto her back. I sat down on the side of the bed and gave her stomach a scratch. I then slid between my 1500-thread count sheets and settled in.

"Are you ready?"

Charlotte indicated she was.

I placed my reading glasses on the tip of my nose, adjusted the light, and opened the book I'd chosen from the bookcase. Charlotte crawled into my lap and began to purr as I began to read aloud. Reading aloud to Charlotte was an activity we both enjoyed immensely, and it was a rare occasion when we missed this ritual at the end of the day. Tonight we were continuing Bram Stoker's *Dracula*. I opened the book to chapter 11.

LUCY WESTENRA'S DIARY

12 September.—How good they all are to me. I quite love that dear Dr. Van Helsing. I wonder why he was so anxious about these flowers. He positively frightened me, he was so fierce. And yet he must have been right, for I feel comfort from them already. Somehow, I do not dread being alone tonight, and I can go to sleep without fear. I shall not mind any flapping outside the window. Oh, the terrible struggle that I have had against sleep so often of late, the pain of sleeplessness, or the pain of the fear of sleep, and with such unknown horrors as it has for me! How blessed are some people, whose lives have no fears, no dreads, to whom sleep is a blessing that comes nightly, and brings nothing but sweet dreams. Well, here I am tonight, hoping for sleep, and lying like Ophelia in the play, with 'virgin crants and maiden strewments.' I never liked garlic before, but tonight it is delightful! There is peace in its smell. I feel sleep coming already. Goodnight, everybody.

I paused and looked at Charlotte. "Perhaps a special Halloween dinner. I'm thinking fondue would be fun. Or maybe a buffet of some sort, where our guests could sample a wide range of offerings. Now that the weather has cooled I've been thinking about digging out the Crock-Pot. Maybe I'll make a soup. I do so love soup in the fall. We could invite Zak and Zoe and their new family, and of course Jeremy and Morgan. Yes, I do believe that will be just the thing."

Our First Dinner Party

There are many things I am certain of, and one of those is the fact that I will forever remember the first dinner party the girls and I threw as a newly formed family. I had never before experienced the sense of belonging that can occur when individuals join together to prepare a meal for those they care about. I invited Mr. Danner, as well as Jeremy and Morgan and Zoe and her family. Brooklyn was happy Pi would be attending, and Pepper asked if she might invite her friend Chad. Surprisingly, Eve wanted to invite Dexter Wilkerson, a student at the Academy who is staying with my good friend Nick Benson, who I invited to come as well.

Before the party the girls and I discussed what to make for our guests. Pepper suggested chili. It seems her mother made chili for Halloween when she was a child. I thought chili sounded like a wonderful idea, but everyone had their own idea of what this chili should look like. Pepper wanted traditional beef with beans, Eve wanted something vegetarian, and Brooklyn preferred chicken to beef. In the end we made three pots of chili, traditional beef and kidney bean, chicken with white beans, and vegetarian black bean. We also made a huge salad, and I picked up three loaves of crusty sourdough bread from the bakery.

"Do you think this is enough broccoli for the veggie tray?" Pepper asked.

We'd decided to serve a selection of sliced cheese and raw fruits and vegetables as an appetizer.

"That's probably enough broccoli, but I'd slice some more carrots," Brooklyn suggested. "Eve has eaten half the ones we sliced earlier."

"I missed lunch," Eve defended herself.

"I washed the grapes when we got home from the market before putting them in the crisper," I informed Eve, who was assembling the fruit tray.

"Why don't you start setting the table?" I asked Pepper. "Let's use the good dishes tonight."

"How many of us will there be?" Pepper asked.

"Let's see. There are the four of us plus Zoe and her family, bringing us up to nine. If you add Jeremy and Morgan that brings us to eleven, Chad makes twelve, and Dex and Dr. Benson and we have fourteen. Oh, and Mr. Danner. We can't forget Mr. Danner."

Pepper and Brooklyn grinned at each other. I know the girls think Will and I have something going on. But we don't. We are just colleagues. Friends with a number of common interests who enjoy spending time together.

The doorbell rang, announcing our first guests, shortly after Pepper and Brooklyn left the room to set the table.

"I'll get it," Pepper yelled.

By the sudden increase in the volume of conversation in the house I was able to infer that Chad had arrived. Chad and Pepper are about as alike as two friends can be. They are both enthusiastic and talkative, with sunny dispositions and smiles that never waver. They are happy and comfortable in any and all social situations, and there isn't a mean bone in their bodies. Both Chad and Pepper are on the cheer squad at the high school, and both freshmen have joined the yearbook staff as well.

Eve and her date, Dex, on the other hand, are about as different as two people can be. Eve is quiet and introverted, with a serious mind and a conservative way about her. She likes literature and classical music and can be found reading during most of her free time. Dex is loud and colorful. He likes to wear wild clothes and his hair color changes from day to day. He enjoys rock and roll and video games during his free time.

"Jeremy is here with Morgan," Pepper informed me as she returned to the kitchen. "Morgan wants to see the kitty. Pepper introduced her to Annabelle, but Morgan seems set on visiting with Charlotte. Is it okay if I take her up to your room so she can say hi?"

"That's perfectly fine."

Annabelle is a small cat Zoe found for Pepper after she expressed interest in having a pet of her own.

"Oh, and Jeremy told me to tell you that he spoke to Zoe a little while ago and they're running late, but only by a few minutes. She had to make a trip to the south shore today and that totally messed up her schedule."

"That's fine. The wonderful thing about chili in a Crock-Pot is that it is ready and waiting whenever you're ready for it. Would you ask Brooklyn to make sure everyone has the beverage of their choice?"

"Yeah, okay." Pepper left the room.

"How did your history project turn out?" I asked Eve, who was preparing the salad.

"Good. The teacher really liked the fact that I took the time to cover both sides of the issue equally. Professor Carlton really had a lot of good input. I'm glad Zak talked him into helping out at the Academy."

"Professor Carlton is a very nice man," I agreed. Ethan is a retired history professor who belongs to the same book club Zoe and I do.

"I asked him if he wanted to come tonight, but I guess he had other plans. Do you think I should add bell pepper to the salad?"

"I think slices on the top would look nice. We have red and yellow peppers as well."

Zoe and her family and Nick and Dex showed up just as Eve was finishing the salad. She went to greet them, leaving me alone in the kitchen with my thoughts for a few minutes as I prepared the oven for the bread. I loved the hustle and bustle of a family, but I had been alone for a long time, so I enjoyed the quiet as well.

I took a deep breath as the scents mingled to create quite a pleasant aroma. In a way, the three young women who I share my life with are like their chili. Each so very different but each complementing the others, so that when combined, they simply work.

"Mind if I come in?" Will Danner poked his head in through the back door.

"Will. What are you doing in the backyard?"

"When I pulled up there were already quite a few cars in the drive, so I parked in the alley. I hope you don't mind."

"Not at all. Come the rest of the way in. I'm almost finished here and then we can join the others."

"Actually, I'm glad we have a few minutes to ourselves."

"You are?" I smiled.

"I've been thinking it might be nice to go to dinner sometime. Just the two of us. Maybe Friday? I know we have Zak and Zoe's party on Saturday."

Was Will asking me out on a date?

"I'd enjoy having dinner with you."

Will let out a breath. Had he been nervous about asking me?

"Did you have something specific in mind?" I asked.

"There's a new steak house on the west shore of the lake. I hear the food is excellent and the view is spectacular. They have live music as well. Perhaps we could throw in a little dancing."

Dancing? As in Will's body pressed close to mine as we moved to the seductive rhythm of a band? I turned my head slightly so he wouldn't notice that my face had most likely turned red.

"You don't like to dance?" Will asked, I'm sure in response to my silence.

"I do. It's just that I'm not really very good at it. I took lessons as a teen, but I haven't had a lot of opportunity to practice since."

"Don't worry. My wife and I used to go dancing all the time. Just follow my lead and you'll be fine."

I smiled again. "Thank you. I'd love to go dancing."

"I'll pick you up at six."

"Six will be fine." I turned to stir the chili, which really didn't need to be stirred. I needed a moment to gather my thoughts. I decided it was best to change the subject. "I'm glad you're planning to attend the party on Saturday. Zoe's parties are always a good time. I even let the girls help me pick out a costume. How about you? Are you dressing up?"

"Actually, I am. I bought a monk's robe from the costume shop when I was in town last week. It is both simple and comfortable."

I laughed. "Perhaps I should go as a nun."

"And cover up all that beautiful hair?"

"I had the best evening," I said to Charlotte as I began my nightly ritual. "Everyone loved the chili buffet. I think the girls and I may have started something. There was even talk of adding a seafood option to the mix for next year's party."

Charlotte sat on the bathroom floor and watched me as I took off my makeup.

"I have to say, I was surprised at the chemistry Eve and Dex seemed to share. I would never in a million years have pegged them as a potential couple. They are as different as night and day and yet together they seem to work."

I applied the first of three moisturizers to my face. My mama had taught me the importance of a religious moisturizing routine and I stick to it to this day.

"And of course Pepper and Chad were as loud and funny as always. I do enjoy their energy. They have a way of lighting up the room and making everyone feel happier. I'm a little worried about Pi and Brooklyn, however."

I began to brush my long, thick hair. One hundred strokes every night keeps it healthy and shiny.

"Brooklyn seems as enamored with Pi as she has been from the first day she met him, but Pi seemed more interested in talking to Jeremy. Of course Pi and Jeremy play in the band together and I know music is important to Pi. And I suppose Pi and Brooklyn are a little young to be in a serious relationship, yet I can see that is what Brooklyn is hoping for. I know her breakup with her last boyfriend was hard on her. I suppose she is ready to move on."

I braided my hair as I always did before going to bed and then began tidying the bathroom.

"Relationships are complicated. I just hope Brooklyn doesn't get her heart broken."

After I was satisfied that I had done everything I needed to do to prepare myself for bed, I set about preparing the room. I worked my way around the area, straightening already perfectly straight books and knickknacks before opening my window just a quarter of an inch.

"Will asked me to dinner on Friday. Although he wasn't specific, I got the feeling he was asking me on a real date. We are even going dancing. I have to admit the thought of dancing with Will brings butterflies to my stomach. It's been so long since I've enjoyed a man's embrace as we sway to the music. I wonder what I should wear."

Charlotte began swatting at the decorative pillows I have stacked on my bed. It was obvious she wanted me to move things along.

"I suppose I'll ask for input from the girls. They are always so good about knowing which clothes best fit each social situation."

After stacking the extra pillows on my white tufted chaise I poured myself a cup of tea from the warming pot I'd already brought up and added a splash of brandy. Then I slid between my 1500-thread count sheets and settled in.

I reached up and touched the end of my long braid. "Mr. Danner said I had beautiful hair."

I sighed as I remembered the thrill of his smile.

After placing my reading glasses on the tip of my nose, I adjusted the light and opened the book we were reading. Charlotte crawled into my lap and began to purr as I began to read *Dracula* aloud. Tonight we would start with chapter 16 of Bram Stoker's masterpiece.

DR. SEWARD'S DIARY-cont.

It was just a quarter before twelve o'clock when we got into the churchyard over the low wall. The night was dark with occasional gleams of moonlight between the dents of the heavy clouds that scudded across the sky. We all kept somehow close together, with Van Helsing slightly in front as he led the way. When we had come close to the tomb I looked well at Arthur, for I feared the proximity to a place laden with so sorrowful a memory would upset him, but he bore himself well. I took it that the very mystery of the proceeding was in some way a counteractant to his grief. The Professor unlocked the door, and seeing a natural hesitation amongst us for various reasons, solved the difficulty by entering first himself. The rest of us followed, and he closed the door. He then lit a dark lantern and pointed to a coffin. Arthur stepped forward hesitatingly. Van Helsing said to me, "You were with me here yesterday. Was the body of Miss Lucy in that coffin?"

"It was."

The Professor turned to the rest saying, "You hear, and yet there is no one who does not believe with me."

He took his screwdriver and again took off the lid of the coffin. Arthur looked on, very pale but silent. When the lid was removed he stepped forward. He evidently did not know that there was a leaden coffin, or at any rate, had not thought of it. When he saw the rent in the lead, the blood rushed to his face for an instant, but as quickly fell away again, so that he remained of a ghastly whiteness. He was still silent. Van Helsing forced back the leaden flange, and we all looked in and recoiled.

The coffin was empty!

"Oh, my." I cuddled with Charlotte. "I'm glad I have you to keep me company tonight. It seems that tales from the crypt are best read during the day."

Charlotte began to purr. Obviously, stories about empty coffins didn't bother her in the least. I continued to scratch Charlotte behind the ears as I read. Eventually, it was the steady rhythm of her purr and not the book that lulled me into a deep and dreamless sleep.

The First Kiss

I will always remember the first real date Will and I shared. My heart pounded right through my chest as he drove me home from our evening together. It had been a magical night I knew I would never forget. The food had been delicious, the music romantic, and the setting enchanting. Will had been funny and entertaining as he told me stories about his life up to that point, and I could feel myself falling in love just a little bit more with each memory he shared. I remember the way my heart stopped beating when we pulled up in front of the house. I'd worried and fantasized since he'd asked me out whether this meal together would end with a kiss.

"I had a lovely time," I stammered.

I could see a movement behind the curtains, so I knew the girls were watching. They'd been so sweet as they'd helped me to prepare for my date earlier in the day. I think in some ways they'd been as nervous as I was.

"I enjoyed myself too," Will replied.

He put the car into park, turned off the ignition, and turned to look at me. He seemed as nervous as I, which was ridiculous considering the man had been married for thirty years and so had logically shared many kisses.

"It seems we have an audience." Will laughed as he nodded toward the house.

I turned and looked at the three faces staring down on us from an upstairs window.

"Yes." I blushed. "The girls were excited that we were going out. I'm sure they waited to hear all about it."

Will took my hand in his and leaned in just a bit. "I'm happy the girls look out for you the way they do. It's a testament to the fine woman you are. But I'd sort of like our first time to be without an audience."

"First time?" I whispered. I felt my body begin to shake, although it wasn't cold in the car in the least.

Will closed the distance between us and gently touched his lips with mine. I closed my eyes as my entire body exploded in a longing I had never before experienced.

Will leaned back just a bit and smiled. He looked at me and his grin grew bigger. "Breathe," he suggested.

I let out the breath I'd been holding. I wanted to be embarrassed that I'd acted like such a fool, totally forgetting to breathe after such an innocent kiss, but Will leaned in and kissed me again, longer and harder, before I could think about it too much.

"Would you like to go out again?" Will asked. "Perhaps a picnic on Sunday?"

"I would," I whispered.

"Good." Will smiled in such a way as to light up his face. "Around noon?"

"Noon would be perfect."

Will looked toward the house again. The girls were still watching from the window. "I guess you should go in. I'm afraid they'll come out after you if you don't."

"Yes," I agreed. "They do tend to be a bit protective."

Suddenly, it hit me that Brooklyn, Eve, and Pepper were the only people in the world to have worried about me since my parents when I was a child. The thought of having people who cared about my daily movements after all these years made my heart feel full and grateful.

Will came around and opened the door for me. He took my hand in his as we walked up the walkway to the front door. I loved the way his large hand felt as it covered my much smaller one. The man was tall and fit and I felt like a schoolgirl as I imagined his wonderfully perfect hands on my body. He paused as we reached the front porch. He turned and pulled me into his embrace.

"This one is for them." He laughed as his mouth met mine briefly one final time before he opened the door and ushered me inside.

"Stop that," I scolded Charlotte as she swatted at my feet while I prepared for bed later that evening.

"Meow."

I stopped what I was doing and looked down. "I suppose I haven't maintained my side of the conversation this evening. It's just that the night was so incredibly perfect that I am afraid if I speak it will break the spell."

Charlotte tilted her head as she listened to what I was saying.

"I know it's silly, but I almost feel as if the night was a dream and the only way to maintain the dream is to be perfectly still, perfectly silent."

I straightened the room after I had moisturized and prepared for bed. I took in a deep breath of the crisp autumn air as I opened the window just an inch.

As I began to sort the decorative pillows I kept on my bed, Charlotte jumped up onto the thick winter comforter and knocked the book we have been reading to the floor.

"Yes, I will read to you tonight. I always do. I believe we can finish the book. And just in time for Halloween."

After placing my reading glasses on the tip of my nose, I adjusted the light and opened the book we were reading. Charlotte crawled into my lap and began to purr as I began to read Bram Stoker's *Dracula* aloud. Tonight we would continue with chapter 25.

I think that none of us were surprised when we were asked to see Mrs. Harker a little before the time of sunset. We have of late come to understand that sunrise and sunset are to her times of peculiar freedom. When her old self can be manifest without any controlling force subduing or restraining her, or inciting her to action. This mood or condition begins some half hour or more before actual sunrise or sunset, and lasts till either the sun is high, or whilst the clouds are still aglow with the rays streaming above the horizon. At first there is a sort of negative condition, as if some tie were loosened, and then the absolute freedom quickly follows. When, however, the freedom ceases the change back or relapse comes quickly, preceded only by a spell of warning silence.

I realized Charlotte and I had already read this passage, so I skimmed down the page to the point where we'd left off. Charlotte didn't care if we reread the same passages, but I found that this evening I was anxious to finish so that I could be alone with my thoughts.

"That I may die now, either by my own hand or that of another, before the greater evil is entirely wrought. I know, and you know, that were I once dead you could and would set free my immortal spirit, even as you did my poor Lucy's. Were death, or the fear of death, the only thing that stood in the way I would not shrink to die here now, amidst the friends who love me. But death is not all. I cannot believe that to die in such a case, when there is hope before us and a bitter task to be done, is God's will. Therefore, I on my part, give up here the certainty of eternal rest, and go out into the dark where may be the blackest things that the world or the nether world holds!"

We were all silent, for we knew instinctively that this was only a prelude. The faces of the others were set, and Harker's grew ashen grey. Perhaps, he guessed better than any of us what was coming.

I paused and looked at Charlotte. I had to wonder if my date was but a prelude to things to come. And although the book predicted darkness, I hoped my own story would be magical and endearing.

The New Forty

In every life there are a lot of usual moments and only a few defining moments. Looking back on my quite ordinary decision to clean out my closet as a way to deal with the sorrow I'd been trying to avoid since Will left I can see that it was that moment when I truly decided to leave the old Phyllis behind and bravely seek the uncertainty of the new.

They say sixty is the new forty. I certainly hoped that was true because I'd just spent the last four hours boxing up all my old lady clothes to make room for the new wardrobe I planned to buy when the girls and I went on our first annual post-holiday clearance shopping spree. I realize that donating 70 percent of my wardrobe is an extravagant thing to do, but the past few weeks have been an emotional roller coaster and I feel, for the first time in my life, that I want to leave my old self behind and invent something entirely new. I haven't worked out all the details yet, but I do know that the Phyllis King who will return to work at Zimmerman Academy, where I am both the principal and a teacher, will be a new and improved version of the sixty-two-year-old who went on break just under two weeks ago.

On the upside of the roller coaster, I had a wonderful Christmas with the three teenagers who now share my life: Brooklyn Banks, a gorgeous and sophisticated sixteen-year–old; Prudence Pepperton, a friendly and energetic fifteen-year-old; and Eve Lambert, a brilliant and introverted fourteen-year-old. We really did have the perfect holiday, and although we are not a real family, I feel that we have started traditions that will endure wherever our paths take us.

Having the girls in my life has given me a new perspective, as well as a renewed enthusiasm for the magic of everyday moments. Who knew how much joy could be had from simple things such as buying trinkets for stockings, singing carols as a family, or working together to create a big Christmas brunch? Prior to the arrival of the girls my holidays had been simple, solitary, and uneventful. I may be a bit late out of the gate, but I feel like Phyllis King the academic is finally blossoming into Phyllis King the woman.

On the down side of the roller coaster is the fact that the one and only man I ever felt I could love has left Ashton Falls to be with his elderly father. I cannot fault Will or his decision to do what he knew in his heart needed to be done. It is a noble man who will put the needs of his family above his own desires. Still, I find that Will has left a hollow place in my heart and an emptiness in my life that I feel an overwhelming desire to fill. The girls are doing their best to keep me distracted, thus the suggestion of the shopping trip in the first place.

"Don't look at me like that," I said to my cat, Charlotte, who was lying on my bed watching me box up the clothes I'd picked out of my closet. "I have not lost my mind. It's more that I've *changed* my mind, and these old clothes no longer fit my new paradigm."

Charlotte rolled over onto her back, a movement that indicated that she was bored with my chatter and wanted her belly rubbed.

I ignored her.

"I'd fallen into such a rut," I continued. "It's almost as if I was sleepwalking through life until the girls came along and woke me up. Not that I wasn't living a perfectly useful life. It's just that my life had become one-dimensional and I'd let it happen."

I held up a wool jacket that was half of a wool dress suit. The skirt would have to go, but the jacket might pair nicely with slacks and a sweater.

"What do you think?" I asked Charlotte.

She jumped off the bed and wandered into my closet, making it clear she really couldn't care less what I did with the jacket.

I decided to keep it to wear with the new jeans and knee-high boots the girls had talked me into buying. It was a good-quality cloth, and the neutral camel color would go with a lot of different things.

I hung up the jacket and then stood in front of the full-length mirror. I tried to be objective as I considered my image. While my hair was still the same waist-length style in which I'd worn it my entire life, the girls had talked me into getting highlights to lessen the gray. My skin was smooth and line free due to a lifetime of rigorous adherence to a moisturizing routine, and I'd managed to keep a slim figure, although lord knew it would do me good to add a toning routine to my day.

"Do you think I should join a gym?"

"Meow," Charlotte commented as she wandered back into the bedroom from the closet.

I took that as signifying agreement.

Between the highlights in my hair, the addition of makeup that Brooklyn had spent hours teaching me how to apply, and the younger and hipper-looking clothes, I really did look as if I could pass for forty, or at least forty-five. I found it hard to remember why I'd never paid any mind to my appearance in the first place.

"I'm thinking that I'll wear my new plum sweater into town. Plum is a good color on me. My mama always told me that plum brought out the sparkle in my eyes."

Charlotte jumped up onto the dresser and knocked the novel I was reading onto the floor. I was certain she was trying to remind me not to lose sight of who I was in the process of reinventing who I wanted to be. Charlotte had a point, but up to this moment I'd lived my entire life in the pursuit of academic achievement and had paid little attention to anything else. I'd never dated, fallen in love, or married. I'd never had children nor engaged in relationships or friendships that weren't related to the academic world in which I'd lived. I'd lived a useful and purposeful life and didn't necessarily regret the choices I'd made, but the opportunity to veer from the path I'd chosen and travel the one unfollowed left me feeling more alive than I had in years.

I changed into my plum sweater, which I paired with black jeans and a soft leather jacket. I picked up the first of five perfectly packed boxes and started down the hall.

"Let me help you with that," Pepper offered.

"I've got this one fine, but there are four more in my room if you want to grab one of those."

I carried the box down the stairs and set it next to the front door. My garage was in the rear of the property, but I decided I'd pull my car up to the front curb, cutting the distance needed to load the boxes in half.

The house, which two days ago had been decorated for the holiday, had been returned to its previous state of tidiness after a long day of undecorating. The tree that had stood in front of the window had been stripped of the ornaments the girls and I had purchased and had been left out on the curb for the garbage truck when it next came by.

I had especially enjoyed all the lights we'd strung: the small twinkle lights that had been added to the garland we'd wound along the banister, the festive red and green candle lights that had graced almost every tabletop, and the larger Christmas lights that had been strung around the windows at the front of the house.

"Are you going out?" I asked Pepper, who arrived with the second box. She had on boots and a jacket, indicating that she planned to venture outdoors.

"Chad is picking me up in a few minutes. We are going to a movie."

Chad Carson was a fifteen-year-old student at Zimmerman Academy and about as close to being a personality double to Pepper as you were likely to find. The two energetic extroverts had been the best of friends from the day they met.

"That sounds like fun," I responded. "What are you going to see?"

"The new action flick that just came out. I can't remember the name, but it's the one with that cutie pie actor Brooklyn is always going on and on about. You can come with us if you'd like."

"Thanks, dear, but I'm planning to head into town to run a few errands. I should be back before you return, but be sure to bring your house key just in case."

"It's in my pocket. Are you sure you don't want to come?"

"I'm sure. You kids have fun."

"Thanks. We will."

After Pepper left the house I went back upstairs for the remaining three boxes. There was a definite satisfaction that came from purging the clothes I'd spent an adulthood collecting, but I experienced a certain nostalgia as well. The sturdy, practical clothing I'd purchased along the way had served me well, even if it no longer fit the new lifestyle I was in the process of designing for myself.

I picked up the next box and headed out of my bedroom. Luckily, I ran into Brooklyn on the stairs, who offered to lend a helping hand. Brooklyn is the eldest of the three and in some ways the hardest to know. She is a perfectly lovely girl, but it is obvious that she has been hurt in the past and therefore guards her heart against future pain by maintaining a barely discernable distance between herself and everyone else.

"Are you going out as well?" I asked as we hauled the three remaining boxes down the stairs.

"Pi is coming to pick me up. He has a gig in Bryton Lake and I'm going to go with him."

Pi was one of the three Zimmerman Academy students living with Zoe and Zak Zimmerman. He was sixteen, as was Brooklyn, and the two seemed to enjoy spending time together, although I think any hope Brooklyn had of entering into a romantic relationship with the musician has gone by the wayside.

"The roads will be icy when you come home," I instructed Brooklyn. "Be sure to remind Pi to take it easy."

"I will," Brooklyn promised as she trotted out the front door.

I looked around the empty house. I knew Eve and Alex Bremmerton, another of the students living with Zak and Zoe, were around somewhere. I doubted they'd want to go into town with me, but I hated to leave without telling them where I was going. If I knew Eve and Alex, they were probably reading or working on a project, so I headed to the library.

"What are you girls working on?" I asked when I found them huddled over a table.

"A treasure map," Eve answered.

"A treasure map?"

"Before we went on break Professor Carlton gave us an extra-credit assignment. We thought it would be fun to try to solve the mystery," Eve explained.

"What mystery?"

"A year or so ago Zoe helped a man named Burton Ozwald find the treasure his grandpa left hidden for his father back in 1940," Eve answered. "All she had to go on was a letter with a riddle, so she enlisted the assistance of Professor Carlton and a few others to help her find the gold."

I did seem to remember something about that.

"Anyway, Professor Carlton thought it would be fun for those of us who had time to try to find the treasure using the same clues that were in the original letter. He hid something in the location where Zoe ended up finding the treasure and the first one to find it will receive a bunch of extra credit points."

"It does sound like fun," I admitted, "but don't you both already have straight As?"

"We do," Alex confirmed, "but the assignment sounded like fun, and a good way to learn more about local history. The thing is, we might have hit a roadblock."

"Do you want some help?" I asked. The assignment really did sound fascinating.

"We can use all the help we can get," Eve answered.

I sat down at the table with the girls.

"Here's what we know so far," Eve continued. "The original letter Burton Ozwald had was really just a riddle that led to an old masthead that was brought to Devil's Den by a man named Warren Goldberg in 1908. It seems he owned a sailing vessel at one time, which he sold to fund his journey west. This article," Eve held up an old newspaper clipping, "says that while he sold the boat to an exporter, he kept the masthead, which held special meaning for him. At some point the masthead ended up in the local bar. That building no longer exists, but during the original treasure hunt Zoe tracked it down to the storage room of the Ashton Falls Museum. Alex and I were able to follow the clues to the museum and, as Zoe had, we discovered a secret drawer. Professor Carlton hid the clue in the drawer in order to replicate the series of events that took place during the original treasure hunt."

I had to hand it to Ethan. He'd certainly gone to a lot of effort to make studying the history of Ashton Falls interesting.

"The clue in the drawer instructed us to look for the medic's seal," Alex continued. "There were a few extra clues I don't believe Zoe had access to at the time of the real treasure hunt, but we were able to track down the information we needed at the library, where a photo of the old clinic was being held for our project. On the exterior of the building was a seal with the words *legatum sit amet*, which is Latin for 'Life Is Love's Legacy.' We can't figure out where to go from there. Professor Carlton did say that Zoe found the treasure, so it seems the riddle is solvable. We just haven't been able to figure it out."

I looked down at the books and materials the girls had spread out on the table. A treasure hunt was just the thing I needed to occupy my mind.

"All right, why don't we start at the beginning?" I suggested. "What was the original clue Professor Carlton gave you?"

Eve pushed a piece of paper in front of me. It read:

> *To begin the quest*
> *I give to you*
> *A maiden's breast*
> *As the initial clue.*

"This is the clue that led to the masthead of a mermaid that had once graced a ship but at some point had been removed and attached to a bar," Eve restated. "As I indicated earlier, at some point it was removed from the bar and given to the museum. When it began to decay it was moved to the storage room, where it still is to this day. This is the clue we found in the secret drawer."

Eve pushed a second piece of paper in front of me. It read:

To find what's next
You must reveal
The hidden text
In the medic's seal.

"I understand that in the original treasure hunt this clue led to the hospital, but I guess Professor Carlton didn't want us digging around in the hospital, so he provided additional clues that led us to the library," Alex added. "A replica of the original photo that was used in the first treasure hunt was waiting for us."

"As we said, when translated the seal says 'Life Is Love's Legacy,'" Eve continued. "We don't know where to go from there."

I looked at the information the girls had gathered. It appeared as if they had followed the clues correctly, yet I wasn't able to figure out what should come next either. "I was planning to go into town to donate the clothes I have boxed up. If you want to come with me, we can stop off at the library to see if Hazel has anything else up her sleeve."

Hazel Hampton is the local librarian.

"I'm in," Alex answered.

"Me too," Eve seconded.

The alpine town of Ashton Falls was busy with shoppers taking advantage of the clear, sunny day as well as the post-holiday sales. I'd planned to do the majority of my shopping at the mall in Bryton Lake, but perhaps I'd check out the local retail outlets as well.

I dropped the boxes of clothes off at the second-hand store that served as a fund-raiser for the local

Food for Families program before heading to the library. Ethan's assignment had me intrigued. Although I'd heard about the outcome of the treasure hunt when it happened, I hadn't been involved and so wasn't privy to the details leading up to the end result.

"Did you girls figure out the clue already?" Hazel asked.

"Actually, the opposite." Eve shook her head.

"We figured out that the seal says 'Life Is Love's Legacy,' but we can't figure out how this will lead us to the next clue."

Hazel held out her hand, indicating that Eve should pass the photo of the old clinic to her. She pointed to the seal. "Do you notice anything else?"

The girls and I all frowned as we tried to figure out what Hazel was referring to.

"Here." Hazel handed Eve a small magnifying glass. "Look at it through this."

"'LIV,'" Eve stated. "It says 'LIV' all in caps on the bottom of the seal."

"So what does that mean?" Alex asked.

Hazel just smiled. I could see she was going to let the girls work on the answer themselves. They took the photo and a pad of paper and headed over to a nearby table. Hazel handed them a box of old clippings, telling them that the answer to the riddle could be found within that box.

"Ethan certainly has gone to a lot of trouble to teach the kids a bit of Ashton Falls' history," I commented to Hazel.

"He seems to be having fun with it, although I think Eve and Alex are the only students still working on it. Most of the Zimmerman Academy kids went home for break, and those who stayed seemed to have other plans. By the way, I was sorry to hear that we lost Will. He was a good man and an excellent teacher."

"Yes," I agreed. "He was. I'm really going to miss him."

Hazel squeezed my hand. We had similar backgrounds in that neither of us had ever married or had children of our own, despite the fact that we adored children. Hazel had been dating Zoe's grandfather, Luke Donovan, for a while now, and it seemed they were getting serious. I hoped that I'd find another man to love. Now that I'd had a taste of what it was like to feel the flutter of awakening desire, I found I rather craved it.

"I think we found it," Eve said. "'LIV' stands for the roman numeral 54." Eve held up an old newspaper clipping. "This article is entitled 'A TRIBUTE TO THE 54.' The article is from the *Chronicle*, and it's dated October 12, 1910. There's a photo of a bunch of men and a couple of women standing in front of the clinic. The article states:

> "'A year ago today fifty-four men from the small mining camp of Devil's Den pooled their meager resources to bring a doctor from our local hospital to their small village to save the life of a prostitute who had developed complications from a late-term pregnancy. Dr. Owen Ozwald, a recently hired resident at the hospital, was chosen for the task. Upon his arrival at the camp,

the doctor found admiration and affection for a community that had come together to save the life of one of their own. Dr. Ozwald was so moved by the commitment of the community to save a single life that he handed in his resignation and announced plans to move his family to Devil's Den in order to open a clinic for those who live in the area. The highly anticipated Devil's Den Medical Clinic opened today and the entire town came out for the celebration. Lilly England, the local madame, who acts as a mother of sorts to the girls, attributes the close-knit community and the willingness of its members to make sacrifices for one another with its isolation from the outside world.'"

"So Mr. Ozwald's grandfather was the local doctor," I realized.

"The thing is, I still don't know how this relates to the next clue," Alex said.

Hazel frowned. "When we got to this point in the original treasure hunt Zoe looked at the photo and made a huge leap as to where she thought the treasure might be hidden, but now that I think about it, we never did actually find the next clue. It seems there must have been one."

I was confused and I could tell by the look on the girls' faces they were as well.

"If you notice in the photo," Hazel elaborated, "the doctor has his arm around the woman on his right. Based on the way she's dressed, Zoe speculated that she was the Lilly England mentioned in the article. She also speculated that the woman on the left with the baby was the prostitute the doctor must have saved. Somehow she made a giant leap from that assumption to deciding that Dr. Ozwald must have given the treasure to Lilly for safekeeping. The next thing I knew, we were heading to the abandoned house Lilly used to live in to look for the treasure."

"Did you find it?" Eve asked.

"We did. The thing is, it never occurred to me at the time that if Owen Ozwald set up a treasure hunt for his son, he would have provided another riddle or clue relating to the seal. I doubt he would assume someone like Zoe would be the one to embark on the hunt for the treasure he left. Very few people could make the leap Zoe did and solve the riddles."

"So we might actually be able to find a clue that has never been found before if we can figure this out," Alex asserted.

"Did you bring the riddles with you?" I asked Eve.

"Yeah." She pulled a piece of paper out of her pocket.

"The first riddle led to a second one, so it makes sense that the second riddle would lead to a third."

I looked at the second riddle again.

To find what's next
You must reveal
The hidden text
In the medic's seal.

"What hidden text?" I asked. "The words *legatum sit amet*, as well as the numeral LIV, are clearly shown on the seal. They were difficult to see from the grainy photo, but at the time Dr. Ozwald planned the treasure hunt, the seal was on the building and clearly visible. There must be a hidden message somewhere on the seal that Ethan and Zoe didn't take into consideration the first time around."

"You make a good point," Hazel agreed. "Let's scan the photo of the seal into the computer; then we can enlarge it on the screen. Maybe there are words hidden somewhere else in the design."

Hazel, the girls, and I looked until we were cross-eyed, but we couldn't find any hidden letters.

"What if the hidden message is within the letters we have?" Alex suggested.

"Like a word scramble?" Hazel asked.

Alex shrugged. "It's just a thought."

"I guess it couldn't hurt to put the clue through the unscramble program I have on the computer," Hazel offered. She pulled the program up on her computer. "If you take the letters from *legatum sit amet* in their entirety, we have quite a few choices, although we don't come up with a single fourteen-letter word. There are several ten-letter words, including *stalagmite*, which fits because Devil's Den was a mining town, and a clue could very well have been left in one of the mines."

"Yeah, but which one?" Alex asked.

"What letters are left?" I wondered.

"U-M-E-T," Hazel answered.

"Mute?" Eve guessed.

"That doesn't ring a bell," I admitted. "Besides, there was no such thing as a computer or an unscramble program back then. It had to be something simpler. Maybe something to do with the translated text."

"Life is love's legacy," Eve repeated.

"Dr. Ozwald wanted to leave his son a legacy or inheritance," Hazel pointed out.

"Maybe Zoe was right all along. Maybe Dr. Ozwald simply arranged for Lilly to hide the gold and then give it to his son when he arrived. Maybe there really isn't another clue," Alex suggested.

"I don't know," Eve said. "The clue leading to the seal clearly states that we're looking for hidden text. Is there another seal?"

"Zoe got the photo we have from Dr. Westlake," Hazel informed us. "She did say he had a whole box of old documents."

"I guess it couldn't hurt to ask him if we can take a look," I suggested.

"Yes, let's." Alex jumped up.

"Maybe we should call Dr. Carlton to fill him in on our plan," I said. "If there is another clue I'm sure he would want to be in on the finding."

Both girls agreed immediately.

I called Ethan, who was, as I suspected, intrigued by our line of thinking. He agreed to meet us at the hospital. Once I'd arranged a place for us to meet, the girls and I thanked Hazel and then headed to the hospital. Luckily, Dr. Westlake was in and agreed to our looking through the boxes of old records and photographs from the clinic at the mining camp.

It turned out there was quite a lot of material to go through, so it was a good two hours before anyone found anything of relevance.

"Look at this." Alex held up an unopened letter that had been closed with a wax seal.

"Who's it made out to?" I asked.

"No one. The envelope is blank. What I found interesting is the seal on the back."

I took the envelope from Alex. The wax seal had the letter *O* in the middle, but what was really interesting was the small words that were so tiny as to be unnoticeable around the outside edge.

"I'm afraid my old eyes can't make out such small type." I handed the envelope back to Alex.

"It says, 'Seek to know for whom the bell tolls,'" Alex informed me.

"The *O* on the seal could stand for Ozwald," Eve said, excitement in her voice. "Maybe this is the seal that was referred to in the letter. Maybe Dr. Ozwald wanted his son to go to a place in town with a bell. Do we have any idea where that might be?"

"The schoolhouse," I suggested.

"Is the schoolhouse still here?" Alex asked.

"I'm afraid not," I answered.

"Phyllis is correct; the old school building has been gone for years," Ethan confirmed. "But the bell that hung in the tower is still around. It's hanging in the bell tower of the church."

"Do you think that bell somehow holds the missing clue?" Eve asked.

"There's only one way to find out," Ethan answered.

We packed everything up and returned it to Dr. Westlake, then headed to the Ashton Falls

Community Church. Pastor Dan was fine with our climbing up into the tower to look at the old bell. Engraved on the side of the bell was one word: *Lilly.* It appeared we'd found the missing clue at last.

The Birthday Mystery

It's my birthday. Although my driver's license insists that I am sixty-three, after all the changes I've made as of late, the three teenage girls living with me tell me I look like I could be forty-three. In the seven months since Brooklyn Banks, Pepper Pepperton, and Eve Lambert have come into my life, I've had my hair cut and highlighted, learned to apply makeup to bring out my best features, and purchased a whole new wardrobe emphasizing the young and hip side I didn't even know I had. At first I was skeptical about making the changes, but I have to admit that when I look in the mirror each day, I really do like what I see.

"So what do you think?" I asked Charlotte, my cat and staunchest critic. "Casual yet trendy or old woman trying desperately to hang on to her youth?"

I was dressed in a pair of straight-legged jeans that were tucked into knee-high leather boots. I wore a knit sweater in a fun pastel shade that accentuated my eyes perfectly. I really hadn't had any grand plans for my birthday, but I also never imagined I'd be spending it attending an orientation for a fitness group. I hoped that my friend Hazel Hampton might want to get together for breakfast, then maybe I'd do some shopping, and perhaps the girls and I could go out for a nice dinner. When I called Hazel she informed me that she had a meeting that morning, but we could try to hook up later. I had my heart set on breakfast in town, so I called my friend Ethan Carlton, who is usually up for anything involving food, but he informed me that he planned to go to the orientation for the new senior fitness group he'd been trying to get me to attend. I have to admit I've been letting my fitness routine slide, and while I may look forty-three, I'm afraid I feel more like I'm eighty-three, so maybe Ethan was on to something.

Joining the local fitness group isn't a decision that comes easily. For one thing it is a *senior* fitness group for men and women sixty years of age and beyond, and I've been doing everything I can as of late to try to look and feel less senior and more middle-aged. Maybe I'm just being silly, but joining a group dedicated to the specific needs of the senior population seems like a step back.

On the other hand, as I age I find my stomach is beginning to droop and my butt is not far behind. Under any other set of circumstances, I might just ignore my sagging body parts, but if I truly want to get back on the horse, as the saying goes, and find a new man to fill the void left when Will moved away, I really should partake in a bit of body maintenance.

For those of you who are unaware, Will Danner was my first and only boyfriend in more than forty years. I don't remember ever consciously making the decision never to date, get married, or have children; it's more that I got busy with my career and the time got away from me. When Will arrived in Ashton Falls I felt my previously dormant heart come to life. Will was younger than I am and he had only recently lost his wife, so I tried not to fall in love with him, but I'm afraid that fall in love with him was exactly what I ended up doing.

I know Will wasn't looking for anything serious, but we did get along, and it seemed that perhaps we might even have a future. Just when I was beginning to believe in happily ever after, Will received a job offer on the other side of the country and I saw the future I'd begun to imagine dissolve before my very eyes.

I know Will gave the situation a lot of thought before deciding to take the job at the college where he was offered a professorship. It was located close to his aging father, who, Will had informed me, was beginning to experience health issues. Will leaving has been hard on me. More than hard. I suppose I wouldn't be exaggerating if I said that on many levels it has been devastating. But I know, like the other heartbreaks and setbacks I have endured in my life, the feeling of emptiness created by Will's departure will likewise pass. It does help to have a full life now that the girls have moved in and occupied the empty spaces in my life.

"Wow, you look great," Pepper commented when I came downstairs. "Are you going somewhere?"

"Senior fitness."

Pepper frowned. "Shouldn't you have on sweats or yoga pants?"

"It's just the orientation, so there won't be any actual exercise today. Where are the others?"

"Eve went into town with Alex and Zoe and Pi picked Brooklyn up. I guess they have plans."

I felt my light mood deflate just a bit. I didn't expect the girls to make a big fuss over my birthday, but I did hope we would all be together. Perhaps Brooklyn had forgotten. It wasn't as if I'd been walking around all week reminding everyone about the big day, but I had marked the date on the calendar we all share.

"I thought maybe we could go to dinner tonight."

"I'm hanging out with Chad today. Maybe another time. In fact, that's him now."

Pepper kissed me on the cheek as she ran out the door.

I felt a sadness overcome me as I looked at Charlotte, who had followed me down the stairs and into the kitchen. Perhaps I should have made firm arrangements with the girls well ahead of time. It's not as if they had known me long and would therefore be expected to remember something so insignificant in their busy lives as the date of my birth. Of course I remembered their birthdays. I'd bought each of them a gift, made them each a cake, and sponsored a small party with their friends so they would know they were loved and remembered.

"It looks as if it's just going to be the two of us again after all."

Charlotte meowed and wound herself around my legs in a circle eight pattern. I supposed it would be fine. I'd spent a lot of birthdays alone. Most of them, if I were to be honest. It's not that I don't have friends; it is more that the old Phyllis really didn't like to make a fuss. In fact, my past five birthdays each have been spent watching an old movie with Charlotte as I sipped a glass of wine and she lapped up a saucer of milk. In the past spending a quiet evening at home was exactly the sort of thing I would have enjoyed. Perhaps it is not just my exterior that has changed over the past year.

Oh, well; what was done was done. The girls had plans and I wasn't going to ask them to change them. Besides, if spending the evening with Charlotte in a quiet house was good enough for the old Phyllis, it would certainly be good enough for the new one. It might be rather nice, or so I tried to convince myself. A quiet evening at home would give me the opportunity to reflect on the past year and make plans for the future.

"Can I have everyone's attention?" Muffy Baldwin, the seventy-two-year-old leader of the fitness group Ethan and I planned to join, began the orientation all new class members were required to attend. I was chagrined to notice that Muffy was in better shape at seventy-two than I was when I was forty-two. Maybe Ethan's idea to join the group had merit after all.

"Let's begin by getting to know one another. It's important in this group that we all support the effort and goals of the others we'll be sharing our time with."

I sat quietly and paid attention as Muffy introduced everyone. There were fourteen people in the room including Ethan and me. I knew almost everyone after having lived in Ashton Falls for quite a few years, but there were a few new faces in the group whose names I made a point of committing to memory.

When we'd arrived I had taken a seat at the front of the room, as I had made a practice of doing over a lifetime in academia, while Ethan had chosen a seat in the back, next to Luke Donovan. I could see they were talking during the introductions, and while I thought it rude not to pay attention while Muffy spoke, they were chatting quietly, so I decided not to say anything.

"There are ten key points to consider when planning a fitness routine," Muffy continued.

She seemed to know her stuff, though I was afraid she was being overly thorough in her presentation. I tried to pay close attention, as I wanted others to do when I spoke, but I found my mind wandering as she rambled on about details that seemed little more than routine.

Not that I'm not grateful that Muffy was so specific in her instructions, but based on the members of our little group, where I'd say the average age was seventy-five at least, it seemed more likely that someone would break a hip while navigating the steps in front of the fitness center than become dehydrated from a long-distance run. Not that proper hydration during distance training isn't important; it's just that in this particular group I found it irrelevant.

I noticed several members of the group begin to nod off as Muffy continued to drone on. Perhaps having us sit while she held the meeting was a mistake. I had a feeling that if she didn't get us all standing and walking around a bit, one or more of the seniors in the room was going to slide right off their chair and onto the floor.

I noticed Hazel sneak in through the side door just as Muffy began to wind down. Talk about perfect timing. She most likely would get credit for attending the meeting because Muffy made a point of waving at her, but she would only be forced to endure a few minutes of what seemed to be an endless monologue. I hoped Hazel would join me in the front of the room, but she sat down in the back next to Luke.

I have to admit I feel a tiny bit jealous of the companionship Hazel and Luke seem to have found in each other. Not that I begrudge them their relationship, but when I watch the way they look at each other I have to wonder if I will ever find the other half of my soul. There are times when I have a deep realization that I've waited too long and am destined to spend my golden year alone.

"Okay, let's review before we wrap things up," Muffy announced.

I tried to focus all my attention on the woman at the front of the room. I'd been an academic far too long not to understand the importance of the postlecture wrap-up. Still, I found my eyes as well as my mind wandering. Brooklyn thinks I should begin to look for a man to replace Will rather than waiting for one to find me. I suppose women in this day and age do oftentimes initiate dates, but I'm not sure I've evolved to quite that degree. At least not yet. Brooklyn told me that I needed to look at men as prospective lovers rather than just as friends or colleagues, which made me blush, but I understand the point she was trying to make. If I wanted a man in my life perhaps I needed to take a more proactive approach.

The minute Muffy excused the group I made my way to the back of the room. "How was the meeting with Zak?" I asked Hazel.

"It went well. We agreed on an extensive library, so ordering the books we need should keep me busy for the next few months. I'm sorry to have missed most of this meeting. How did it go?"

"It was long and you didn't miss much. Do you have plans for the afternoon? I thought maybe we could all have lunch."

"Actually," Hazel widened her glance to include myself, Ethan, and Luke, "I was sort of hoping the three of you would have time this afternoon to help me with my little mystery."

"Mystery?" I did love a good mystery. Perhaps this birthday would be a little more exciting than I'd first imagined.

"Do you know the Hornwell house on the edge of town?"

Ethan, Luke, and I all confirmed that we did.

"It seems the court finally settled the probate and it sold a few months ago to a lovely family. The new owner brought a box of books into the library last week that had been left in the attic by the previous owner. He didn't want them and hoped to donate them."

I waited for the punch line. So far a box of books from an old house that had been boarded up for ten years or more since Edith Hornwell passed didn't make for a mystery.

"Anyway," Hazel continued, "I found what I initially thought was a personal journal among the books. When I looked more closely at the journal, I realized it was actually a novel written out in longhand. I read it and loved, it so I overnighted it to a friend who works as an editor for a publishing house. She indicated that they were very much interested in publishing the story if we can find the author, or the heir if the author has since passed, and work out a contract. The main problem is that the only information we have as to the identity of the author is the name Anna B."

"When was the book written?" I wondered.

"In 1956."

"So the author most likely has passed unless she wrote it when she was very young," I pointed out.

"I suppose there's a good chance the author has passed, but if she was, say, twenty when she wrote the book she'd only be eighty now. I know it's a long shot, but I thought it would be fun to try to track her down."

"I guess it would be fun to do a little sleuthing." I found myself being pulled into the mystery. "What's the book about?"

"It's the story of a woman who marries an older man when she's just a teen and then leaves everything behind to start a new life in the west. The story is set in that latter part of the nineteenth century, and in many ways it's a common story as historical romances go. In my mind the thing that makes it stand out is that the woman who wrote the novel had an exceptional grasp of both human emotion and motivation. When she describes the hardships and heartbreaks her heroine endured, you can easily make the leap to what many women experience in everyday life even in the twenty-first century. How women lived a hundred years ago is very different from how they live today, but how they *felt* about the challenges and sorrows in their lives is very much the same."

"It sounds like a wonderful book. Did you keep a copy?" I asked.

"No. But I'm sure my friend will return the one I sent her when she's finished with it. Anyway, I got a sub for the library today because I had the meeting with Zak and wasn't sure how long it would take, but we finished up early so my day is wide open. Are you interested in joining me in a little investigation?"

"I'm game for whatever you want to do." Luke put his arm around Hazel and gave her a brief squeeze.

"Sounds like a good way to spend the afternoon," Ethan agreed. "I might even have some documents at the house that will help. Edith Hornwell was a force in the community for a lot of years. There were quite a few news articles written about her, and I happen to have a copy of a biography that was published about her maybe twenty years ago. If the journal was found in her attic she must have known the author and maybe she's mentioned."

"I'm in as well." I smiled.

"Let's all head to my place," Ethan suggested. "We can have lunch while we come up with a game plan."

Ethan lives in a lovely home, although it is very much a bachelor pad. It is decorated in dark colors with hardwood furniture that is a bit austere for my taste, but his library is absolutely fabulous. The floor-to-ceiling bookshelves frame a warm and inviting room where it is easy to imagine whiling away a winter day or a lazy summer afternoon. Ethan seems to spend a lot of time in the room, as evidenced by the worn sofa along one wall, a cozy chair near the fire, and a long table completely covered with books.

After asking his housekeeper to prepare a light lunch of fruit and sandwiches, Ethan instructed us to head down the hall toward the library. He cleared the table of the books, then instructed us to take seats while he gathered the materials he thought we'd need. As it turned out, Ethan had already done quite a bit of research about Edith Hornwell, which I found both helpful and suspicious. Suspicious of what I really didn't know, but given the fact that Hazel had just informed us about the manuscript and the mystery, it seemed a tiny bit too convenient that Ethan had the documents he would need close at hand.

"Is there anything we already know about Edith that might help us choose a direction for our research?" I wondered.

"I've actually read up on the woman, as I have many of the original families," Ethan informed us. "I can't claim to know who Anna is or how she might or might not be related to Edith, but I do have a basis from which to initiate our study."

Ethan informed us that Edith had first moved to this area in 1930, when the town was known as Devil's Den. She was just twenty at the time she moved to the mining camp with her new husband, who owned the general store. The couple were wealthy by local standards, so the house her husband built was one of the largest around. Ethan reported that, based on what he had read, the couple seemed quite happy with their lives and their marriage, in spite of the fact that they'd barely known each other prior to the wedding arranged by mutual friends.

It seemed odd to me that Edith would not only marry a man she'd only met a handful of times but would move across the country, giving up everything she knew to do so, but Ethan informed me that Edith's father was an abusive man and, in his opinion, she'd been faced with two less than desirable choices and had chosen the lesser of the two evils.

Edith and her husband had four children, all boys. Her sons, as well as her husband, all predeceased, so when she passed in 2006 at the age of 96, the only heirs left to inherit her estate were distant relatives she had never met. The house stood empty until the past year, when it was sold to the man who'd donated the books to the library.

I thought it was important to remember that Devil's Den had turned into little more than a ghost town in the 1940s before it was redeveloped by Ashton Montgomery a decade later. While most residents had left the area during that time, there were a few who stayed through the transition, and Edith was one of them.

According to Hazel, the novel she found was dated 1956, so the person who wrote it would have lived in the area during the initial phase of the redevelopment of Devil's Den to Ashton Falls. That is, assuming the person who wrote the novel lived in the area at all. We were just speculating at that point that the author was known to Edith in some way, perhaps even staying in her home. It was entirely possible that Edith had gained possession of the piece of writing in some other way.

"So Edith would have been forty-six when Anna wrote the novel. We know Edith only had sons; could Anna have been a daughter-in-law?" I asked.

Ethan opened the biography. "According to this, Edith had four sons. Her oldest son married a woman named Lily Belltree and had three sons of his own. He second son married a woman named Carolyn Kingsley and they had two daughters, Beatrice and Angelica. I suppose it's possible Anna could be a nickname for Angelica." Ethan turned a few pages and then turned back a couple, as if looking for something specific. "No, it looks like Angelica would only have been six in 1956, so it couldn't be her."

"And the others?" I asked.

"Son number three was killed in a riding accident as a young man and never married and son number four married a woman named Glenda Wall who apparently was barren. They adopted two sons. There don't appear to be any Annas in the family tree that I can see. At least not in the immediate family. Edith had seven sisters, so it's possible Anna could be a sister, or a niece perhaps?"

I sighed. "As far as I can tell, we have two big problems. First of all, the novel is simply signed Anna B. Anna is a common name, and the B could stand for anything, so I really don't see how we are going to be able to track this person down even if she has not yet passed, which, given the fact that it has been sixty years since the manuscript was written, seems more likely than not. Our second problem lies in the fact that the novel was written so long ago that anyone who might have had firsthand knowledge of this Anna has most likely moved on or passed on. I'm not sure where to begin."

"It would be easy enough to see if Edith had a sister or niece named Anna, I suppose," Hazel offered. "I've helped several people create family histories over the years and you'd be surprised how much information is readily available on the Internet if you know where to look for it. Chances are Edith's sisters are all dead but there might be a niece."

"Ethan has an extra computer in the den if you want to take a look I can help," Luke offered.

Hazel looked at Ethan.

"Fine by me. There are a few people in town who lived in the area in 1956. Maybe we should just ask around to see if anyone remembers anything."

I hadn't lived in Ashton Falls that long so I didn't know which of our neighbors Ethan might be referring to, but Luke came up with a name right off the bat: Burt Pollin. Burt, like Edith, had lived in the area prior to the redevelopment and stayed on when the others left. Luke wasn't certain of his age, but we all agreed he had to be in his midnineties.

I suggested we call Burt to ask if he remembered an Anna who might have either stayed with or been friends with Edith, but Luke suggested we speak to him in person; he was going deaf and a phone conversation might be tricky. Luke called and made an appointment with Burt's son, who had moved in to help care for his elderly father, while Hazel headed down the hall to log on to Ethan's spare computer.

I decided to thumb through the biography, while Ethan saw to the final arrangements for lunch. It seemed that Edith was an opinionated and outspoken woman who had ruffled more than a few feathers in her day. She was an advocate for women's rights long before that was trendy, and she was well known in the community for temporarily taking in women escaping abusive relationships. That actually fit in with the fact that she had been abused herself.

It dawned on me that perhaps Anna was one of the women Edith had rescued. I wasn't sure how we could confirm my suspicion, but I was having a wonderful time. While delving into a mystery was the furthest thing from my mind when I woke that morning, I found I was captivated by the story and really wanted to solve the mystery. This birthday, I decided, would be the best I'd had in quite some time.

I'd only managed to make my way through a fraction of the book when Ethan called us in for lunch, which, by the way, was fabulous. Either Ethan normally dines on lobster sandwiches on fresh bread, fruit salad, and hearty clam chowder, or he somehow knew to expect company. I do at times tend to be the suspicious sort and wonder if there might be more going on than might appear on the surface, but I was having a wonderful time and the food was divine, so I decided to set my suspicions aside and enjoy the day with my friends.

Like Edith, who had lived in the same house for most of her life, Burt had lived in the home he now shared with his son since the days the area had been known as Devil's Den. He was in remarkable shape physically given the fact that he'd recently celebrated his ninety-second birthday, but his hearing was starting to go and he didn't like wearing a hearing aid, so we had to shout loudly to be heard.

"What is that you say about Gwyneth? Is she okay?"

"No, Pop, not Gwyneth." Burt's son, Lance, explained that Gwyneth was his niece's new baby. "They want to ask you about Edith Hornwell."

"Thought the old biddy finally up and kicked the can."

"She did pass away, quite a while ago. They want to ask you about a woman named Anna who may have been friends with or might possibly have lived with her at some point."

"Edith had boys. Four of them. All strapping young men as dumb as their papa and as muleheaded as their mother. Don't remember no girls. Pretty sure Edith was much too sour to produce any girls."

"What about someone in the community named Anna?" Ethan shouted so as to be heard. "Someone who would have lived here in 1956."

Burt screwed up his face. "There was an Anna who worked at the bar. Pretty sure she was a hooker. Might have been after 1956, though. The years, along with the memories, all seem to fade into a single block of images when you get to be my age. Now Elvira, there was a woman who left a lasting impression."

"Elvira?" I asked.

"Someone Pop knew in his youth," Lance explained. "He talks about her quite a lot. More and more often as time goes by. I think she must have been some great yet tragic love from early in his life. I'm not sure Pop can help you. His memory is fading and he really never liked Edith, so the two weren't friends. In fact, they seemed to have quite a rivalry going over something that happened at least sixty years ago. I never could get a clear answer from Pop as to what started the whole thing, but he really hated the woman quite a lot. Have you spoken to Maude Collins? I know she moved to the area in the early fifties and she would most likely have been around twenty in 1956. Maybe she knew this Anna."

"Okay," Luke shook Lance's hand. Then he turned to Burt. "Thank you for taking the time to speak to us."

"Have you lived in the area all this time?" I wondered. Lance was probably in his mid-to-late sixties, based on his appearance. He was a good-looking man who I would think I would have noticed prior to this if he'd lived in Ashton Falls for any amount of time.

"No. I left town when I was a young man and only moved back about a year ago to help out when Pop had a fall and needed round-the-clock care. It was clear Pop would need live-in help for the remainder of his days and I'd recently retired and didn't really have any ties where I was living, so I moved home."

"Your father lived alone until last year?" The fact that the man had lived alone until he was ninety-one was downright amazing.

"He had day help, a maid and a nurse who checked on him a couple of times a week. But yeah, until the fall he was mostly self-sufficient."

It was stories like this that gave me hope that I too would be self-sufficient well into my golden years.

We chatted with Burt and Lance a few minutes longer and then headed toward the car. Hazel made a quick call while Luke, Ethan, and I decided what to do. It was still early, so following up with Maude seemed a logical choice should we be able to contact her about an interview. Luke called and made the arrangements. As expected, she was happy to speak to us.

When we arrived at her home we were greeted with tea and pastries that she must have had on hand. As Burt had, she continued to live alone in spite of her age, and it appeared she was still as sharp as she had ever been.

Hazel quickly explained our purpose for being there.

"Edith did take in several women over the years. None of them stayed long. It seemed she provided them with temporary refuge while they made plans to leave their abusive situations." Maude paused as she tapped her chin, as if deep in thought. "I don't remember anyone named Anna, however. Of course the women Edith housed more often than not kept to themselves. I suppose that's understandable, given their situation. I only met a couple of them and then only briefly, so it's possible this Anna could very well have been one of Edith's rescues."

"Do you know if Edith kept any records concerning the women she helped?" I wondered. It would make sense she might keep something concerning their arrangement to fall back on should she need to explain or defend her involvement with these women who were obviously escaping very volatile relationships.

"I'm not sure. Edith was a very deliberate woman, however, so it wouldn't surprise me in the least. Have you asked the new owner of the house if he came across any records of this type while cleaning out the attic?"

I looked at Hazel.

"No. I just spoke to him for a moment when he dropped off the box of books, and at that time I didn't know about Anna or the manuscript."

I frowned. Something was definitely up. It would seem that the first thing Hazel would do if she wanted to find this Anna was to ask the new homeowner if there were photos or other references to a woman with that name.

"I guess following up with him would be a good idea," Hazel added.

I glanced at her with a look of confusion on my face that earned me a sheepish look in return. If I had to guess, there was something going on that had nothing to do with a novel Hazel loved so much as to go to all this effort but didn't even bother to keep a copy of. I glanced at Ethan. Could this be Hazel's way of arranging for Ethan and me to spend more time together? After Will left town Hazel had casually commented that Ethan and I might make a good pairing. Could this whole investigation be nothing more than an elaborate blind date?

"You know," Maude added after a pause, "there was one girl who stayed with Edith around the time you're asking about. I never met her, but I did see her in the yard a time or two. She was a tiny little thing. I'm going to guess she was around fifteen or sixteen. I don't remember if Edith ever mentioned her name. She never went out in public and only ventured into the yard early in the morning or late at night. I imagine she wanted to avoid the curious stares of her neighbors. Edith's youngest son was still living at home at the time. I remember wondering if the girl wasn't his girlfriend. Of course Edith's sons are all gone, so I suppose there's no way to inquire as to the relationship, if there was one."

"Perhaps someone else in the community will remember more about the girl. Thank you for your time. I think we really should be going." Hazel seemed to be wrapping up the conversation somewhat abruptly considering the fact that we were all still sipping our tea.

"But you just arrived," Maude complained.

"Yes, but I have a meeting to get to this evening and I just received a text that it's been moved up."

Meeting? What meeting? We'd been together all afternoon and Hazel had never once mentioned a meeting.

After we left Maude's house Hazel excused herself to make a quick call. I assumed our next step would be to arrange a visit with the new owner of Edith's house, but when Hazel returned she announced that she really needed to be going and suggested we pick this up another day. We'd all driven in Ethan's car so we returned to his home, where Hazel and Luke quickly said their good-byes and left.

"That was strange," I said to Ethan.

"Strange how?"

"I don't know. We spent the whole afternoon trying to track down a woman who may or may not have lived in the area sixty years ago and all of the sudden Hazel had to leave after Maude made an excellent suggestion about speaking to the man who bought the house. Frankly, I would think speaking to the person who donated the books in the first place would have been the first thing Hazel would have done. The whole thing seems pretty odd to me."

Ethan shrugged. "Been single my whole life. There isn't much a woman could do that I would understand."

If this whole day had been some sort of fix up on Hazel's part she most definitely was barking up the wrong tree. Ethan was a nice-looking, intelligent man, but when it came to women he was about as clueless as one could be. I couldn't help but compare him to my Will, who always knew the perfect thing to say and do to make the woman he was with feel like the only one in the world.

"I don't suppose you'd want to grab some dinner? My treat." I figured that even if I had to pay, dinner with a friend was better than dinner alone on my birthday.

"Actually, I have plans. Maybe another time?"

"Oh. Okay. Another time."

I walked out to my car and tried to fight the tears that seemed to come from nowhere. What was wrong with me? I'd spent the majority of the birthdays in my life alone with my cat and never once become weepy over the situation. I suppose living with the girls had created expectations that an old woman such as myself had no right to have. I unlocked my car and stepped inside. I adjusted my mirror, buckled my seat belt, and turned the key in the ignition. Nothing.

Perfect. Just what I needed to wrap up my day. I got out of my car, walked back to Ethan's front door, and rang the bell. When he answered I noticed he'd already changed into a very nice shirt and slacks.

"Sorry to bother you, but my car won't start. I was wondering if you could give me a jump. It seems I have a dead battery."

Ethan poked his head out the door. "I'm already late. Maybe I can just give you a ride home and we can deal with the car later."

I really hated to leave my car, but Ethan did look like he was ready to go out and I hated to keep him, so I agreed. I had two vehicles, actually—a classic my dad had left me and my Volvo—so I would be able to get around if I needed to.

"Thank you. I would appreciate that."

I couldn't help but notice that Ethan smelled good as he helped me into the car. I imagined his plans must be with a woman. Ethan really did look nice when he took a minute with his appearance and I couldn't help but feel a tiny bit of envy for his mystery date.

"It was fun to spend the day with Hazel and Luke," I chatted as we made the short trip to my home.

"Yes. It was a good day."

"And lunch at your house was lovely. I'm not sure I took the time to properly thank you."

"My pleasure."

"It's too bad Hazel had a meeting to get to. I'd hoped she'd be free for dinner."

"Humph," Ethan sort of grunted, as if he didn't have the energy to reply but felt he should respond in some way.

"It's my birthday today." I'm not sure why I said that. I really hadn't planned on mentioning it.

"It is? Happy Birthday. I guess you need to get home to get ready for evening plans as well."

"Yes. I suppose the day has gotten away from me."

We pulled up in front of my house. The sun had set and I could see there weren't any lights turned on inside. I guess the girls still weren't home.

"Well, thanks again for the ride. I'll see to the car tomorrow."

Ethan parked the car and got out. He opened my door for me and walked me up the sidewalk to my own front entry. I turned the key and began to step inside.

"Surprise!" pretty much everyone I knew shouted.

I placed my hand over my heart to slow the jolt it had received from the shock. I noticed Ethan was holding my elbow to help support me.

"A surprise party? For me?"

Brooklyn, Pepper, and Eve all ran forward and hugged me.

"Were you surprised?" Pepper asked as she jumped up and down in typical Pepper fashion.

"I was. My heart is still pounding. Did you girls to all of this?"

"With Zoe's help," Eve confirmed.

"But I thought you had all forgotten my birthday."

"Are you kidding?" Brooklyn plopped a pointed hat on my head. "You're like our mom now. We could never forget. We love you and are so grateful to you for taking us in. We just wanted to show you how much you mean to us. Happy Birthday, Phyllis."

By the time the party wound down and everyone left it was well past midnight. I should have been exhausted, but somehow I felt energized as I entered my room to begin my nightly ritual. Charlotte sat and watched me as I began removing my makeup and moisturizing my skin. My mother, God rest her soul, had drilled into my head the importance of a proper cleansing and moisturizing routine when I was still a young woman. She'd taught me the structured ritual I follow to this day.

"I will admit the day has held its share of surprises. I still can't believe so many people went to so much trouble to surprise me on my birthday. Zoe and the girls did a wonderful job with the food and decorations, and Hazel, Luke, and Ethan all gave up their entire day to keep me occupied while the girls got the house ready. Even Maude, Burt, and Lance were in on it. Can you imagine? I've never felt so special."

I slipped a nightgown over my head and then began sorting the clothes I had removed. I hung those that could be worn again on hangers and separated those that needed laundering into differing baskets.

"I'm sure this day will go down in history as one of the best in my life."

Charlotte yawned. She appeared to be communicating that she had bored with my chatter. I ignored her.

"And the best part about it was that while I assumed that Hazel had made up the whole mystery just to distract me, it turns out everything we discovered was true. The only part that was fake was that Hazel pretended not to have found Anna when actually she had weeks ago. She must have done exactly as Maude suggested and gone to speak to the new owner of Edith's home the day she read the manuscript. He was more than happy to let her dig through the boxes of paperwork Edith left behind. Once Hazel had a full name and date of birth for Anna, she'd asked Zak to help her track the woman down." I set the decorator pillows to the side before fluffing the one I slept on. "It turns out Anna was only fifteen when she wrote the book, which, based on what Hazel had to say about the quality, is simply amazing."

Charlotte jumped onto the bookshelf as if to remind me that we were due to start a new book tonight. I stood in front of the colorful bindings, trying to decide.

"It seems Anna's father was physically abusive and her mother died as a result of his abuse. She stayed with Edith for a summer while they sorted things out. In the end she went to live with an aunt.

According to Hazel, she forgot about the novel but very much wants to have it published. Isn't that amazing?"

"Meow."

I made my choice and settled onto the bed. I pulled the comforter over my legs.

"Are you ready?"

Charlotte jumped up onto my nightstand, knocking a package off onto the bed. Ethan had handed me a gift as he was leaving and I never had gotten around to opening it. I'd brought it upstairs with me when I retired for the evening but had waited to open it.

"The gift." I smiled at Charlotte. "Of course I should open the gift."

I carefully removed the wrapping so as to extend the moment. I don't know what I thought might be inside, but I certainly wasn't expecting the book hidden within the wrapping paper.

"*Pride and Prejudice*. A first edition."

Charlotte was more interested in the wrapping paper than the book, but I was overwhelmed by Ethan's generosity. He and I had been chatting about novels a few months earlier and I had mentioned that *Pride and Prejudice* was my all-time favorite. A tear slid down my cheek. I couldn't believe he'd remembered. Perhaps Ethan wasn't as clueless as I'd thought. It took a man who was very perceptive to know what lies within a woman's heart.

Recipes

Recipes from Kathi
Cheesy Potato Soup
Fettuccine Alfredo
Snowball Cookies
Triple Chip Cookie Bars

Recipes from Readers
Date Nut Bars—submitted by Taryn Lee
Orange Balls—submitted by Pam Curran
White Fudge—submitted by Jeanie Daniel
Pumpkin Bread—submitted by Sharon Guagliardo

Cheesy Potato Soup

My mom made this almost every year on Christmas Eve.

12 cups potatoes, peeled and diced
1 bunch leeks or green onions, washed and chopped
8 cups chicken broth
4 chicken bouillon cubes

Boil until potatoes are tender. Mash potatoes into small chunks in broth. Do not drain.

Lower heat and add:

1 cube butter
1 8-oz. pkg. cream cheese
2 cups heavy whipping cream

When cream cheese is completely dissolved add:
8 cups cheddar cheese, shredded
2 cups of Parmesan cheese, grated
Salt and pepper to taste

Simmer until cheese is melted and soup thickens.

Notes:
Add cheese slowly, stirring constantly until blended.
You can add broccoli, cauliflower, or both for variety.

This soup makes a *lot* but is good as a leftover. In fact, many times Mom made the soup the day before, refrigerated it, and then reheated.

Fettuccine Alfredo

This is another Christmas Eve favorite at our house.

Melt 1 stick butter (real butter, no substitutions) in saucepan over medium heat.

When melted add:
½ 8-oz. pkg. cream cheese
2 cups heavy whipping cream

Stir until cream cheese is completely dissolved.

Slowly add:
1½ cups Parmesan cheese, grated (the good stuff)
1 cup Romano cheese, grated (add slowly; don't let it clump)

Stir until smooth.

Add:
1 tsp. ground nutmeg
½ tsp. garlic powder

Add salt and pepper to taste (Ellie uses white pepper).

Note: if you like your sauce thicker you can add additional Parmesan and if you like it thinner you can add additional cream.

Pour over fettuccine, tortellini, or any other pasta (fresh from the refrigerator section is best).

Snowball Cookies

Mix thoroughly:
2 cups softened butter
1 cup powdered sugar
2 tsp. vanilla

Stir in:
4½ cups flour
1 tsp. salt

Add:
2 cups chopped walnuts

Refrigerate at least 1 hour.

Roll into 1-inch balls and place on ungreased baking sheet. Bake at 400 degrees until set but not brown. While still warm, roll in powdered sugar. Let cool and roll in powdered sugar a second time.

Triple Chip Cookie Bars

Graham cracker crust:
3 cups graham cracker crumbs
¾ cup melted margarine
½ cup sugar

Combine and press into 9 x 13 baking pan.

Middle layer:
½ cup chocolate chips
½ cup butterscotch chips
1 can (14 oz.) sweetened condensed milk
1 tsp. vanilla

Microwave for 1 minute; stir, microwave 30 seconds more. Pour over crust.

Topping:
Remainder of large bag of chocolate chips (approx. 11 oz.)
Remainder of large bag of butterscotch chips (approx. 11 oz.)
1 cup white chocolate chips
1½ cups salted peanuts

Pour evenly over crust. Bake at 350 degrees for 25 minutes.

Date Nut Bars

Submitted by Taryn Lee

This is my great-grandmother's date nut bar recipe. My mother loved to bake at Christmastime and this was a family favorite. I remember our baking time together with great fondness. There were always date nut bars, divinity, fudge, red and green M&M cookies, and cut-out sugar cookies to be made. There wasn't a year that went by that she didn't makes this recipe, and now that she's gone, my sister makes it because it was always her favorite. I still have my mother's handwritten copy of the recipe, stains and all.

¼ cup Wesson oil (you can use whatever oil you have)
1 cup brown sugar
2 eggs
½ tsp. vanilla
¾ cup flour
½ cup chopped nuts (we usually used pecans or walnuts or a mixture of both)
1 cup finely cut dates
Powdered sugar (to roll bars in)

Mix Wesson oil and brown sugar. Add eggs and vanilla; beat well. Add dry ingredients and stir well. Add nuts and dates. Put in oiled 8 x 8-inch pan. Bake at 350 degrees for 30 to 35 minutes. Cut in bars and roll in powdered sugar.

Orange Balls

Submitted by Pam Curran

This recipe came from an ex-sister-in-law, Annette. She gave it to us a long time ago. She used to make them at Christmas. I don't know where the recipe came from, possibly her mother. But it has been a family favorite during Christmas.

1 box powdered sugar
1 stick oleo/margarine
1 can (6 oz.) frozen orange juice
1 box (12 oz.) vanilla wafers
1 cup chopped pecans
1 can coconut (about 8 oz.)

Pour slightly softened orange juice over crumbled vanilla wafers. Leave until soft. Add softened margarine and powdered sugar. Mix and shape into balls. Roll in coconut. These are best kept in the refrigerator until needed. They can be frozen, but you may not have any left to keep in the freezer.

Note: You can color the coconut to match any holiday. I also make these at Halloween on occasion and just use the green cherries, then color the coconut orange.

White Fudge

Submitted by Jeanie Daniel

This is a recipe for my sister's white fudge. She only made it at Christmas, and when I was a child I would eagerly await the arrival of the fudge. I would savor each bite. It just melts in your mouth, so good! It was my daddy's very favorite thing for Christmas. She finally gave me the recipe years ago. Now I make it at Christmastime in my daddy's memory.

2¼ cups granulated sugar
½ cup sour cream
¼ cup milk
2 tbs. butter
1 tbs. light corn syrup
¼ tsp. salt
2 tsp. vanilla
1 cup candied cherries, quartered
1 cup walnuts, chopped

Combine sugar, sour cream, milk, butter, corn syrup, and salt in a heavy 2-quart pan. Stir over moderate heat until sugar is dissolved and mixture reaches a boil. Boil over moderate heat for 9–10 minutes or 238 degrees on a candy thermometer. Remove from heat and allow to stand for 1 hour until mixture is 110 degrees. Add vanilla and beat until mixture loses its floss. Stir in cherries and walnuts. Put in a buttered pan. I use a glass 8-inch square pan.

Pumpkin Bread

Submitted by Sharon Guagliardo

1½ cups flour
½ tsp. salt
1 cup sugar
1 tsp. baking soda
1 cup pumpkin purée*
½ cup olive oil
2 eggs, beaten
¼ cup water
½ tsp. nutmeg
½ tsp. cinnamon
½ tsp. allspice
½ cup walnuts, chopped

Preheat oven to 350 degrees. Whisk together the flour, salt, sugar, and baking soda.

Whisk the pumpkin purée, oil, eggs, ¼ cup water, and spices together, then combine with the dry ingredients, but don't mix too thoroughly. Stir in the nuts.

Pour into a well-buttered 9 x 5 x 3-inch loaf pan. Bake 50 to 60 minutes until a thin skewer poked in the very center of the loaf comes out clean. Turn out of the pan and let cool on a rack.
Makes one loaf. Can easily double the recipe.

* To make pumpkin purée, cut a pumpkin in half, scoop out the seeds and stringy stuff, lie face down on a foil or Silpat-lined baking sheet. Bake at 350 degrees until soft, about 45 minutes to an hour. Cool, scoop out the flesh. Freeze whatever you don't use for future use. Or, if you're working with pumpkin pieces, roast or boil them until tender, then remove and discard the skin. I use Libby's canned pumpkin.

Books by Kathi Daley

Come for the murder, stay for the romance.

Zoe Donovan Cozy Mystery:
Halloween Hijinks
The Trouble With Turkeys
Christmas Crazy
Cupid's Curse
Big Bunny Bump-off
Beach Blanket Barbie
Maui Madness
Derby Divas
Haunted Hamlet
Turkeys, Tuxes, and Tabbies
Christmas Cozy
Alaskan Alliance
Matrimony Meltdown
Soul Surrender
Heavenly Honeymoon
Hopscotch Homicide
Ghostly Graveyard
Santa Sleuth
Shamrock Shenanigans
Kitten Kaboodle
Costume Catastrophe
Candy Cane Caper

Zimmerman Academy The New Normal

Ashton Falls Cozy Cookbook

Tj Jensen Paradise Lake Mysteries by Henery Press
Pumpkins in Paradise
Snowmen in Paradise
Bikinis in Paradise
Christmas in Paradise
Puppies in Paradise
Halloween in Paradise
Treasure in Paradise – *April 2017*

Whales and Tails Cozy Mystery:
Romeow and Juliet
The Mad Catter
Grimm's Furry Tail
Much Ado About Felines
Legend of Tabby Hollow
Cat of Christmas Past
A Tale of Two Tabbies
The Great Catsby
Count Catula
Cat of Christmas Present – *November 2016*

Seacliff High Mystery:
The Secret
The Curse
The Relic
The Conspiracy
The Grudge

Sand and Sea Hawaiian Mystery:

Murder at Dolphin Bay
Murder at Sunrise Beach
Murder at the Witching Hour

Road to Christmas Romance:

Road to Christmas Past

Kathi Daley lives with her husband, kids, grandkids, and Bernese mountain dogs in beautiful Lake Tahoe. When she isn't writing, she likes to read (preferably at the beach or by the fire), cook (preferably something with chocolate or cheese), and garden (planting and planning, not weeding). She also enjoys spending time on the water when she's not hiking, biking, or snowshoeing the miles of desolate trails surrounding her home.

Kathi uses the mountain setting in which she lives, along with the animals (wild and domestic) that share her home, as inspiration for her cozy mysteries.

Kathi is a top 100 mystery writer for Amazon and she won the 2014 award for both Best Cozy Mystery Author and Best Cozy Mystery Series.

She currently writes five series: Zoe Donovan Cozy Mysteries, Whales and Tails Island Mysteries, Sand and Sea Hawaiian Mysteries, Tj Jensen Paradise Lake Mysteries, and Seacliff High Teen Mysteries.

Giveaway:

I do a giveaway for books, swag, and gift cards every week in my newsletter, *The Daley Weekly* http://eepurl.com/NRPDf

Other links to check out:
Kathi Daley Blog – publishes each Friday
http://kathidaleyblog.com
Webpage – www.kathidaley.com
Facebook at Kathi Daley Books –
www.facebook.com/kathidaleybooks
Kathi Daley Teen –
www.facebook.com/kathidaleyteen
Kathi Daley Books Group Page –
https://www.facebook.com/groups/5695788231468
50/
E-mail – kathidaley@kathidaley.com
Goodreads –
https://www.goodreads.com/author/show/7278377.
Kathi_Daley
Twitter at Kathi Daley@kathidaley –
https://twitter.com/kathidaley
Amazon Author Page –
https://www.amazon.com/author/kathidaley
BookBub –
https://www.bookbub.com/authors/kathi-daley
Pinterest – http://www.pinterest.com/kathidaley/

CPSIA information can be obtained
at www.ICGtesting.com
Printed in the USA
BVHW040825190320
575431BV00007B/144